OTHER SIDE OF MEKONG

Somsy Camvan

PublishAmerica
Baltimore

First printing

Photo used in cover art provided by Denise Pickett.

Softcover 9781462652846
PUBLISHED BY PUBLISHAMERICA, LLLP
www.publishamerica.com
Baltimore

Printed in the United States of America

Chapter 1

It was a June night, at the Mekong shore when my problem of love relationship that involving crime started. Six years had passed since my girlfriend was killed by cluster bombs while we were student my love for her remained unchanged. The woman who was soon to come into my life would act as remedy. Until she found a wealthy and powerful man and began dividing her love between us. When the truth was brought to my attention, my whole life became a song of calamity. I met her shortly after I had arrived on other side of the Mekong in Thailand. But before that I was living in fear of police would send me back to Laos. I thought finding a partner would be my best chance to being sent to a refugee camp and having my name put on the waiting list in order to have opportunity to be sent to third country, and never had a second thought that a tragedy would happen again.

At first, the new woman I met at police station and having a relationship with for the next several years risked her own life to save mine. She would become a secret mistress to the governor, or maybe that is not the reason, so much as that she desired revenge, wanting to kill the police officer who raped her a year before, I could not be sure. In any case, she put aside our future together. The last note she wrote from her prison cell said: I would like you to be there on the day I am hanged. I wanted you to know, I left to save you; I was dead inside long ago. All that matters now is you. I never attached myself to a man before as

I did with you. This leaves out any chances to relationship back. From that day on until these days it has always been a calamity in my mind that I should not deepens relationship and be free of internal complication.

Before swim across the river to on other side, I had boarded the 6 am bus from the capital city, Vientiane, on its way direct to Pakson, some hundred-seventy kilometers. Because it was a dirt road, the bus could only travel at twenty or thirty kilometers per hour, so after a long day of travelling, we arrived an hour before nightfall. As the bus stopped, I ran into the bulrushes and hid, waiting for darkness to come that I could swim across the Mekong to the other side in Thailand. I remained still in one spot to avoid being spotted by police patrols. I hoped that once I reached the other side the next day, I would meet up with some people, but never thought that such a complicated love relationship was in store for me.

The heat and humidity of the month of June began to die down. The evening breeze still carried hot air down to me, but then the cool air came at last. The river was red, as it was all year. It looked muddy, but people drank from it. As I got thirsty, I put my hands together and scooped the water to drink from time to time. Drinking a lot of water helped to slow my hunger. However, I needed energy to swim across the half-mile span of the river in order to survive, so I pulled out some bulrush roots and chewed on them to fill my stomach. To make my body lighter I took off my clothes, gathered them in a bundle and attached on my head and I jumped into the river and swam across.

CHAPTER 2

Although I was among those who reached the Thai shore and made it to the town police station, I was not feeling safe. The town had a reputation as a home of criminals, though its population was not large. In the past, it had been known as a popular canoe-dock, and a trading market between Laos and Thailand. But, the market had closed long ago, after the communists took over Laos. As the border fell into disuse, the dock also closed; the only markings of the past were the old poles that remained sticking up from the ground above the tall bulrushes. From a distance, it looked as though there were people standing with their heads above the tall grass here and there. The whole area had been tranquil since everything closed.

The shore has no trace of humans, coming to launch canoes as they used to, or grazing livestock. On the ground along the shore were tall grass and bulrushes, and stretching as far as the eye can see. The wild plants had grown which gave an impression of the place having been abandoned for long time. It almost felt as though one was far from the civilized world, as there were no signs of people, apart from myself, and perhaps other refugees who had been there before me.

The rumors before I even cross the border were spreading that now more criminals were returning to the area for new potential, for new prey: the refugees. They would rob or rape the women before they let them go to the police station, killing them if they resisted. Police were assigned to protect their own Thai citizens first, until they received an order of the United Nations to bring in reinforcements to protect the refugees. Following that, the police would at least help the refugees who had already registered and had their names put on the list in the United Nations registration books, but even so, they too were often involved in the rapes, and in some cases would sell the young women to brothels.

June was a season of rain; the grass and other plants made a landscape that was green everywhere. The natural beauty did not give me or any of those around me any fresh feelings, we were seeking refuge and fearing what was to come. The bushy grass was almost silent, as if it too were standing by itself far from civilization. Since the place was no longer useful, I thought, chances were that it would become wild again, even though it was located only a thirty-minute walk from the town police station. There, beside the domestic criminals being held temporarily in cells awaiting court hearings, there were now many refugees awaiting their new status, and I was soon to be among them.

I sat on the ground waiting for the dawn to emerge. There were not many natural sounds, not even noise of rapids from the river, which would have helped to occupy my mind and reduce my anxiety about the possibility of being assaulted by the Thai criminals or even by the police officers. We had all had heard that the officers were full of hatred and were angry about the refugees flocking into their town and country every day. From the sea came Vietnamese people known as boat people, from the land came Cambodians fleeing from Pol Pot regime and from the river came us. We were escaping from the unfair treatment we had lived though in Laos and the rapidly deteriorating economic situation, my case was even more frightening, I was accused of leaking undisclosed information to western medias.

It was so dark that I was unable to see in any direction, I sat on the ground through the hours before the light of the dawn could be seen and I could make my way to the road above. Once in a while, I heard the sound of leaves of grass sanding against one another from the force of the soft near-morning wind. I found myself in a place I had heard about as a place of opportunity for a long time, both for people from Laos and Thailand, a place to make a living by selling and buying home-grown commodities. But now things had changed: those relationships no longer existed. I was feeling tired but unable to close my eyes, when fear knocked again as I thought I could be handcuffed for entering Thailand without proper documentation. From my experience with authority, I had always found them to be manipulative, no matter what a political regime that state is constituted. I hoped that the Thai police would not take my coming to Thailand to escape the atrocity personally, that they would understand the situation I was in: being vulnerable, a lost child, and having come here for safety and freedom and to make the best of it all.

The sun rose. The shore was filled with water, mixing with the mud. The river was rising from the rain a few days ago. I stood up, looking into the distance to determine west, which was where in I knew I had to walk. Finding it, I saw many rooftops in that direction. I bent my head so that it would be below the level of the grass, and, to avoid the long grass leaves cutting my face, extended my arms out to the front and walked. I walked on the black, sandy soil through the grass to the road which ran along the river. The paved road was clean but full of cracks and potholes; cars and tricycles were speeding past one another from both directions. The drivers and pedestrians paid no attention to me or my strange look. I was wearing a white t-shirt, blue jeans, soaking wet, and was empty-handed. When the traffic slowed, I crossed the road and found myself at the edge of the town. I made my way along a dusty trail through a mango bush and as I reached a small dirt road before the main street, I saw an old man riding an ox-cart. When he saw me, he stopped his cart and pointed to the west.

"The Bung-gun police station is three blocks from here," he said, "Go! And tell them the truth." Without looking at me again, he pulled the rope that tied to his ox and melted away toward the west.

Whatever was in the old man's mind, I chose to take his words as assistance, coming from human compassion. I walked as I had been told, "three blocks from here to the west."

I reached my destination in less than fifteen minutes, spotting the police station sign. The building was constructed in the style of a private house: there were two storage rooms with cement floors, wooden walls, and wooden siding painted brown. And as I went inside, the whole first floor was made up of offices. The second floor was all cells; each cell was closed with an iron door like a black garden gate. The cells were divided into single rooms and each had an access door to a hall on each side and there was an office at the end of the hall. The office had a desk, three chairs and a telephone. There was no filing cabinet, no piles of paper. There were always two officers there, watching the cells, their eyes like those of a lion watching his prey.

After I was inside the building, pausing to look at the work schedule on the wall to the left of the entrance, which said that the office opened at 8:30. The clock above the schedule read 6 o'clock. There was no light in the office apart from the natural rays of the morning sun being sent through the windows. The night shift officer appeared.

"You must wait," he told me, before going back to his box-like office. As he disappeared, the whole building seemed to fall silent. It was only at that moment, as I stopped moving once again, that suddenly I felt tired. I leaned my back against the wall beside the door, my eyes suddenly difficult to keep open, and fell asleep.

It was as though something was turning on and off in my mind, without fully sleeping. As I opened my eyes again, something caught my attention through the window. I pushed my arms up, my knees still on the floor, and put my chin on the windowsill to look out into the street. There was a group of students heading west on bicycles: the girls were wearing white shirts with short sleeves and blue skirts, which were almost miniskirts, falling above their knees. The boys wore the same white shirts with short khaki pants. Both boys and girls were wearing blue bandanas around their necks. The students were talking to each other as they pedaled, but I could not hear their words. I was thinking of an encounter of my own. I was a student once, earning my college degree and later contributing to society a great deal as reporter, but now those good things in my life were gone. My thoughts turned further back, to the memory of my younger and poorer years living with my adopted single mother, who left me too young, leaving me to survive school on my own, which was a constant struggle.

After a moment, the students I had admired disappeared, and the street remained. There were only ox-carts pulled alongside streets, tuke-tukes carrying merchants to morning market, and transport trucks making a loud noise one after the other. Then the road was empty again. This pattern repeated itself through the time I spent waiting for the office to open. I found myself in a place and situation where I could do nothing; I was waiting for something to come. I wasn't sure what would be a good thing, other than seeing a police officer, but he might then turn out to be a manipulator of some kind and throw me in a jail cell. I told myself grimly that I should not think like that.

When the light came on, I realized that there were more people on the second floor than I had thought. There were police officers, refugees and a gang of robbers which had been brought in the day before. Everyone inside the cells wanted their words to be heard; the prisoners' talk echoed through the building like the sound of the morning parakeets in the deep jungle. Then, the caretaker rolled up the curtains, a set of keys hanging from her belt made noise which kept me awake as it came to my ears. She began rolling up the blinds, and before long sunlight shone into the building.

I stood by the door, anxiously watching her go from place to place, carrying out her duties, and when the she passed, I said, "Excuse me; I would like to report myself to the police." She did not stop walking, but replied, "You are not the only one, you have to wait," and she went up to the second floor. Afterward, I realized that I should not ask her that, the police man had told me that a while ago and the working hours sign was on beside the entrance.

A tall, dark man with a thick black mustache walked in through the door. He wore a blue t-shirt with an alligator embroidering on the left above the chest. The bottom of his shirt was tucked into his gray pants. A handgun was on the right-hand side of his waist. As he opened the door, I felt a draught of warm air from the outside. The man looked serious, calm, serene and dignified. As I was waiting, anxious to be called, or maybe handcuffed, a group of men entered and walked through to his office and remained there for more than thirty minutes. At the time, I had no idea who they were, but would find out the following Monday, when I saw a large group of them come to pick up refugees and take them to the camp, that they were contract drivers.

The caretaker emerged from the second floor staircase, and without speaking, extended her arm toward a door marked with a number eight. I thanked her, but she did not wait to receive my thanks, walking away instead and that was first and last time I saw her.

After the drivers had left the room, I went to the door. The dignified officer was on the phone, but when he saw me at the door, he gestured for me to come inside. I went in and he put the phone back in its cradle and told me to close the door. "Have a seat" he told me. His desk was made of gray metal, with a small lower bar on the side closest to the wall. There was a black typewriter on the desk, and beside the typewriter was a pile of file folders about a foot high which looked as though it was about to fall. He did not say his name or extend his hand for me to shake, however I saw his name written on a plaque on his desk: MR. PRAYUNE VANNARANE.

"What is your name?" he asked. "Bo, nicknamed B," I replied. "I'm not interested in your nickname," he said harshly. "What did you do in Laos?" he then asked. I told him that I was a reporter. "Reporter?" he repeated. His face was still red, but his rude attitude had stopped. He mumbled and typed a half-page. He commented: "It is a good job, why did you leave?" I told him that there were many reasons: the censorship of my work, living conditions and the constant suspicion under which I was living, and the consequences: no freedom of expression, accused of making friend with western journalists. He continued typing in silence, not making eye contact.

Finally, Mr. Vannarane stopped and stared at me. I saw then that the mood which had appeared at the beginning had changed. His tone of voice had become less rude as he continued to question me. He asked for my place of birth, personal interests, education and goal for the future and if I was a member of Lao communist party, after I said no he then took my fingerprints. He explained the procedure in Thailand for refugees, and spoke about the supervision by the United Nations of refugees in Thailand before applying to go to the western countries. He said that all the information I had given him about myself would remain on my personal file at the police station and a copy would be sent to the refugee camp in Noug khai, to remain there until my departure from the country. He didn't shake my hand before he sent me out.

"Leave the door open," he said, raising his voice once again. I walked out and back into the hall. I sat on the floor beside the entrance. My clothes had begun to dry, but my back was itchy. I sneezed once in a while and felt terribly sleepy, but not for long: one of the officers took me to a cell on the second floor.

He told me that I would have to stay in the cell at night until I was transferred to the camp, but that I was free to come and go during the day.

Chapter 3

On my third day at the station, I was not feeling well. I had pain all over: my neck, my back and head were aching. When the officer opened the cell, I went to and take a shower and then put my clothes back on, the only ones I had. At least they were dry, but they had mud stains on them, especially my jeans. I didn't notice this until I took them off: it looked as though I had made a patch and stuck it on purpose to cover a hole. I made an effort to wash them off, but since I only had one set of clothes I didn't want to try too much and get them too wet, so I left them until the next day.

The hot sun was shining down on the rooftop. The temperature was still rising, having reached perhaps twenty-five or thirty degrees, and the sun reflected off the cement and the tin roof, making the air even hotter. I stood beside the hedges, still looking for a shady spot to sit, when I felt a draught behind, and as I turned to look, I was facing to a woman, she asked me: "Did you just arrive today?"

"Yesterday," I said. I wasn't sure if it was her had seen the day before, sitting on the cement curb, but wasn't in the mood to talk to a stranger. The woman smiled, but not a fully expressing of happy smile. Her mood showed some relief from agony after I engaging my words with her, and we began to chat. "I got this side of the river a week ago," she volunteered but told me latter that she just comes to the station yesterday.

The woman looked about twenty-one, or twenty-two I could not be sure. As I standing beside her I found her height was less than me several inches, something like that. Her face had a beautiful natural coloring: pink lips, black eyes, brown and red, ripe-mango cheeks. Her outfit was plain; she was wearing jeans, and through her t-shirt I could see her white bra and erect breasts. Her look impressed me, given the situation we were in: her clothes were plain, but she looked so striking. I suddenly had a feeling of compassion between us. As I explained myself, speaking my mind, she began to cry, first softly, but then the sound began to rise until she could no longer control it and she started to walk away. I followed her to a shed and sat beside her. I wasn't sure what to do then just listen to what she had to say.

"I am Nang Ya," she began. "I am a second-year student at Dong Doke University in Laos in the teaching program. After I escaped, I swam with two of my friends across the Mekong. Halfway across the river, I could not hear one of the girls anymore. The other girl and I could not return to look for her; we carried on to the shore. Once we were there, we realized that our friend hadn't made it. We sat at the shore for an hour crying"

"The next morning we walked to the police station and reported ourselves. That evening, instead of bringing us to our cell, the young policemen took us to the canoe-racing festival to the south about thirty minutes drive from here and we partied there until midnight. Then two police officers took us to the rice warehouse, I don't remember where it was. We went into a dark room and there were many men, more than five. After finishing drinking something like whiskey, I don't remember anything more until I woke up the next morning completely naked. The warehouse employees brought me to this police station and just brought me to a cell. This was yesterday, the same time as you, I guess."

"My cell is number seven," she said. She told me to wait for her while she walked back to the building. "I will be here." I said. She nodded her head and ran off. I saw there were many police officers who had arrived for work. Many came by bicycle and the others by motorcycle. About less than fifteen minutes later, she came out of the building. She stood facing me, slid her hand under her t-shirt and pulled out a handful of cash. "I sold my gold necklace. It was a gift from my father for my high school graduation," she explained. "We are going to find something to eat."

At first I was struck by this. I had told Nang Ya that lunch is at noon at the station canteen, and she also knew that from before she met me. But, she insisted on having the food of her choice. My need for a companion was great and her personality was well-suited. I agreed, but admitted that I had no money.

We went to the food-market. I wasn't sure how far it was from the station, but it didn't seem to take us long to get there, especially since we were talking constantly. The market was made up of two buildings about a hundred feet from one another. Between them was a large open space with a paved floor and large umbrellas in a row. Under each umbrella was a stand with wheels underneath, from which was sold anything ranging from noodle soup to a full range of Thai cuisine in various cooking styles? In the two buildings, which had tin roofs; meat, live chickens, fruits, vegetables, and many other commodities were being sold. There was a mixed smell in the air: fresh fruit, cooking aromas and live fish and chickens.

We ordered two large bowls of noodle soup. The woman brought the bowls and put them on the counter. "I put extra meatballs for your boyfriend, no extra charge" said the woman. Nang Ya looked at me with emotion and added pepper and chili sauce to my bowl before hers as the woman turned away. While we were eating, she grabbed a rag that was lying on the counter and wiped off a piece of noodle stuck to my chin. Once in a while she looked at me for a long time. I haven't had any kind treatment from women for a long time. Now it was a like a new medicine that would ease the pain of loneliness. Nang Ya seemed to be truly feeling the need to build a relationship with me, just as much as I was looking for someone in my life, someone to share obstacles and joy with me again. My teenage years were long gone and I hoped this thing would work between us.

After we had finished eating, we needed to find a way to get through the crowd. We had to walk sideways sometimes to avoid bumping into people. To avoid losing each other, we held hands. I walked ahead of her and she held my hand, twisting my arm. We walked until we got to the curb at the east entrance of the prison. But before we got there, along the edge of the street we had taken to go to the market, there were carts lined up, one after another, and they were selling all kinds of bread: long baked sticks of French bread and cookies and other Western desserts. Nang Ya let go of my hand and turned to the carts. She selected some bread and asked: "Which one do you want, Bo?" I walked to her. "I like what you like," I said. She smiled and picked up four baguettes.

It wasn't the norm for a girl to pay for lunch for a boy. However, given the unusual circumstances, my man's ego was already far from the norm. Now, something had happened that might bring comfort or might help to build a long-term relationship, so I allowed myself to take whatever role came with it. In this situation, the beliefs and the dignity which culture had taught me were a given had become an ideal. I was no longer keeping with my free child ego, but instead adopting an adult destination of whatever that maybe.

When we got to the station, a police officer told us that our departure would be confirmed that afternoon. He suggested that we should be aware of that and should come to the meeting where departures would be announced in which would be in the canteen. He didn't give us a time. We were anxious to have the confirmation, and went to sit on the cement curb outside, leaning against one another. It was another new norm to build a relationship in one day, but we were going with our instincts.

"Mr. Vannarane told me to find a roommate; minimum of one, maximum of six," she said. The refugee camp was run on limited space; it could not allow one person per room because the refugee population was increasing by the week and because it was easier to categories applicants if they were grouped together. I told her not to worry.

"He tells everyone one the same thing, but I'm not sure if the camp will allow men and women who are not married to share a room," I said. She turned to face me, looking anxious and sad. She couldn't express her feelings, and dropped her head shyly.

As matter of fact, there was no rule, nor religion that would guide us to live in a proper manner at the moment in the camp.

After many of the officers had returned from lunch, they called us to the meeting over a crackling loud-speaker. We were standing outside, in front of the entrance. Mr. Vannarane stood in front of the closed door and announced: "Those of you who have seen me this week and have signed up for refugee status will be transferred to the permanent camp in Nongkhai on Monday, unless your record needs further investigation, in which case you will remain. The team of UN aid workers will come tomorrow morning to give you all basic necessities and to conduct a final interview." He ended the announcement by congratulating all those who had reached safety and avoided any loss of life, and then turned and went into his office.

A bit later, Nang Ya and I were still chatting when a policeman came out of the station and called me inside. "See you later," I said to her. I followed the officer inside and he slowed down to walk behind me and then pushed my back to direct me to the second floor. He took me to cell number four. He opened the gate and pushed me into the cell. After the gate was locked, the officer walked away. I grabbed the Iron Gate, standing still and watching him walk away, short while later a policewoman came past escorting Nang Ya. As they passed my cell, Nang Ya gave me a signal: "Pats up seven fingers," which meant cell number seven. They took us into our cells to make space outside.

My cell was above the staircase and I could see people as they went up and down and they could see me. I was sharing the space with a gang of robbers. Most of the time I didn't stand at the gate with my hands on the bars, since there was often one of my fellow inmates occupying that space, I often sat on the floor in the corner with my arms around my knees. My mind was hungry most of the time because there was nothing to read in the cell, all I had to do was wait and watch people going up and down the staircase. As the time moved toward late afternoon I grew hot and felt eager to have a shower. The officers were treating us roughly that day, making us go to our cells before sunset because it was too crowded outside. It was also too noisy, as people who had seen their names on the list that waiting to be called were calling out to their friends and cellmates, letting them know that their plight was over, at least on the first step.

The bathroom was at the end of the hall, there was only one for both the men and the women. Although there were more than ten showerheads attached to the wall, having a shower was an act of waiting. They opened the women's cells first and I saw the women flock to the shower room. About fifteen minutes later they began trailing out one by one, the stream of women continued for more than an hour. Then the officers opened the men's cells, they did first one half of us and then the other, because among the men there were not only refugees, but criminals as well.

At supper, I joined Nang Ya. We had to walk to the extending building where the dining room was, with the long kitchen behind it. Along the wall, near the entrance, there were many water taps on the ends of rusty pipes. We were only allowed to use plastic cups, no glass or metal was allowed. I felt as though I were part of a herd of buffalo or a criminal that committed a terrible crime; we were no longer individuals, just a group being moved from place to place commanded by police.

When we sat down to eat, I realized that Nang Ya was not wearing any makeup. Her natural skin was smooth and slightly dark and her long, black, shiny hair hung down her back. Smiling did not come naturally to her, the only time she smiled or laughed was when she deliberately did so. She had found out that wearing miniskirts was forbidden in police custody, she wore blue jeans as usual since I met her and a white shirt instead. The jeans were tight, giving her the look of a teen-aged school girl. She spoke in a soft tone, always making sure that her listener was paying attention while she spoke, and she was immediately silent when someone else spoke. She kept looking into my eyes while we talked. My mind was undeniably occupied throughout the supper, listening and also sharing my thoughts, feelings and experiences with her. Our conversations were filled with joy and took our vulnerabilities off our minds, until we had to change to more serious subjects. I came to learn that her communication skills were well above average; when I spoke to her, it always created a feeling of joy and inspiration in me.

It was nearly the end of supper when she asked me another question. "Have the station guards ever given you any trouble? They told me not to wear anything short that came to above my knees." I told her that they hadn't. "They are not allowed to give us any trouble, remember? We are not criminals, we are refugees and are protected by the United Nations," I said. She argued, "There are no UN workers here now, the Thai police can do anything they want until they send us to the permanent camp, don't you think?" She put her blue plastic cup on the table. A kitchen worker came and told us to move, she needed to clean the table. It was time to go back to our cells, and as we stood up, Nang Ya took hold of my hand.

She always looked into my eyes, but when I looked deeper, I saw something that hinted that I was not the one. I might be in her mind for the rest of her life, but there was something else lurking there, something that needed to be finished. "I'm glad I met you," she said as we walked out of the room. The guard opened my cell; as usual he pushed my back as I walked in. Before I sat down in my usual spot, the criminal who I shared the cell with gave a loud "Ha!"

"My friend, I saw you holding hands with that sexy girl, is she your girlfriend?" I remained silent. The three men who were in the same cell had robbed the jewelry stores in town the same night I arrived on the shore. They had been arrested on the scene and were being held until further investigations could be done. I told the first man that she was not my girlfriend, that I had only met her yesterday.

Then I sat down, leaning my back against the wall, silent once again. The man moved over to me, "What's the matter? You're supposed to be happy, I just saw you holding hands with your girlfriend," he said, "don't tell me she isn't yours, soon you will be out of the Iron Gate and you can fuck her again. Don't you ever think about that? She is hot, I tell ya!" He laughed to himself and his two colleagues looked at me and one said, "Don't take it personally, he's crazy." I stood up and walked to the gate. The man who had just spoken handed me a cigarette. "I don't smoke thanks." Outside the gate I saw a policewoman looking at us. "I'm just trying to make this young man feel at home, okay miss?" he said. "You're right," said the officer, "If he wants to talk to you, you can talk to him, if he doesn't, then leave him alone, okay?" She walked away with her keys dancing noisily on her belt, her mind on other things, her own world.

"Okay, miss. You are beautiful." He ended this by blowing her a kiss. She ignored him and walked over to another cell. The man finally introduced himself to me as Prince Salaherlandsran. He was tall and skinny but very masculine, with dark skin and eyes that never made contact with anyone when he spoke.

I had the impression that the officers did not take the criminals seriously; the relationship between them was full of jokes, which was funny to me. I felt less fear now than before. Now that I realized there wasn't any danger of harm from the criminal, I engaged him in conversation. He found it difficult to lie down on the floor, most of the time he sat with his back against the wall, saying Buddhist prayers or singing. Those were his daily activities, apart from picking on people.

The target of his teasing for the moment was me. The other two didn't do much of anything apart from watching us as well as the busy traffic which passed through the hall outside our gate. Most of the time my cell-mates were silent, but sometimes they talked amongst themselves, discussing how to answer the officers' questions when they were brought down to the interrogation room on the first floor. It was odd, though, that when the men spoke among themselves, they spoke in Thai and when they spoke to me, they spoke in Esane. Esane is the Lao language, and has a strange accent. Hundreds of years ago, all the Thai districts along the Mekong belonged to Laos, and that when Thailand invaded and claimed the districts as theirs, the language of Laos continued to be used for the spoken word, although Thai was used or anything written.

The hall was dark, but the prince kept a light on the lower part of the wall turned on. I didn't want to move from my spot, uncomfortable though I was, in case I should bump into him.

He asked why I had made my mind up to escape from Laos, especially given he job I had at the newspaper. When I explained to him that my life had been in danger due to the political situation, and that I had left without regret, he nodded his head in empathy. I didn't ask why he decided to be a robber, but he volunteered the information anyway, to pass the boring times, I guessed.

As the prince told it, he was employed by a sugar cane farm for eight years before his arrest. Three years after he began working there, he fell in love with his boss's daughter, who was still attending college, studying agriculture. Each weekend when she came home, he would show her how to harvest the raw cane and taught her about processing in the factory. In return, she taught him high-school material and urged him to find time to finish his diploma. As the relationship grew, they began having sex. At first he said it would only be for a while, but as time went on she was sneaking out of the campus during the week. They would meet at a local hotel, or at a friend's apartment, or at the movie house.

"I thought of marriage, and of inheriting her father's farm and the factory, but after she got pregnant, her father had me sent to jail," he said. I heard the sound of him trying to control a runny nose, though I couldn't see his tears in the dim light. I remained silent.

"I wasn't looking for trouble," he explained, "it was only because I loved her, but her father pressed rape charges against me and I was in jail for three and a half years. You know, many people talk. My son was four years old, but I wasn't allowed to see him. My parents told me to leave town and never return. I left, and got a job at Marova Na's house in Bangkok, selling things to tourists until I was arrested again for trafficking drugs. This time, though, I had money and could pay for the time I was supposed to be in the cell. After they released me, I gathered myself a gang. We would break in and steal jewelry and high-valued merchandise from stores, but we never robbed banks."

"Robbing banks is just like stealing from you," he said, "most of the money in the banks comes from poor people. This time they arrested me for stealing three hundred thousand bath's worth of watches from a store just a few blocks from here, two days ago." I wasn't sure if he was telling me this because he wanted my advice or just to express his restless thoughts as he contemplated the questions he would be asked about the crime.

The gang was taken to the first floor for interrogation the next morning. An hour later, they returned to the cell, the prince had blood under his chin. I looked at him but did not ask. His eyes were stretched wide open and he was staring at the gate. When one of the officers passed by, he shouted, "Those sons of whores hit me!" I was silent. "Ha! Say something, my friend, I am talking to you!" I looked at him again, afraid that he might punch my nose in his anger. I asked, without thinking, "Which sons of whores do you mean?"

He shouted, "The policemen and women, you know they joined the force because they don't have mothers, and they get angry about their lives and they hit good people. With the last senseless remark, he burst into tears. To me, whatever the reason was for the police officers hitting him, it was frightening. It seemed that torture was still a common practice here.

I remember once, my history teacher said, "People with less education spend the most time insulting others, and give themselves a new status." I imagined that Salaherlandsran had named himself a prince and spent a lot of time insulting the police. Afterward I felt lucky, for walking a path in life which was acceptable human behavior. For those who walk on a non-existent line, taking peoples' belongings and harming them, there were consequences to be faced which created negative emotions within themselves and caused them to speak in unpleasant language, and eventually fall to disgrace. Even if they were given knowledge later on, it would have little impact.

I thought about Nang Ya after the end of my conversation with the Prince. Nang Ya had almost graduated from university and would have been comfortably settling into the teaching profession by now. She had left for a better life, or at least that was what she believed. Soon, as a refugee, she would enroll on a waiting list to go to Western countries. Alone, by herself, could she make it to her destiny and desires? With that thought of her, I asked myself as well, could I make it? If not, what were our lives to be ahead?

Chapter 4

There were six hours of interviews before it was my turn the day the UN team finally arrived. I wasn't sure how many refugees the officers interviewed that day, but I was the last to enter the room where they were seeing people. They did not call people in alphabetical order; it was first-come-first-served. I was anxious to be served first, but I was not aggressive enough to push through the crowds to be the first, inconsequence, I ended up being last.

Nang Ya and I had not made arrangements to be interviewed at the same time. I was thinking of her, but was not sure how to go about it. In reality, we were strangers, we had no commitment to share our lives in the future, and it seemed that circumstance had brought the relationship into being on its own. When Nang Ya got to the door, she did not go into the room, caught in a sudden uncertainty. I looked her in the eyes. "I am sorry," she said, "if you don't want me to come with you I can go in after you." She appeared distressed, she wasn't sure if we should go in right away and call ourselves a couple, or wait and tell them later in the permanent camp. As the last couple in front of us, who had three children, went in, I took her hand and held it tightly in mine. She looked into my eyes, her tears dripping. For better or worse, I thought, I have a companion. I felt calm, relaxed and optimistic with someone beside me who appeared to care for me, I started contrast to my non-existent family life when I was young. "What are we going to tell them?" she asked. In her eyes there was only curiosity, and doubt about what I could tell the officer about how we were connected, there was no judgment, no challenging of my opinions, whatever I might say.

"I will tell them that you are my girlfriend," I said, "Is that okay with you?" I could feel her hand shaking. I turned and kissed the top of her head. She put her arms around me, with her ear against my chest. "It is okay with me, yes." The couple came out, the husband carrying a sheet of paper, and walked back to their cell. "I wish that my two friends could be here, along with me, that I could introduce you to them." I could imagine her emotion; I too always had a desire for friendship which would last for a long time, and which would somehow create happiness and confidence which would improve my moral worth.

Her hand was soft and warm, and as I held it, emotions began to rise in me, and without thinking, I turned and kissed her passionately. She wrapped her arms around me and kissed me back, without any words being spoken, our love relationship had been born at last. I was nearly overcome with elation at our mutual passion. The officer called, "Next!" I walked in on the left, Nang Ya on the right. "How are you?" asked the officer. I was impressed that the officer took a civilized tone, given the circumstances, most officers were not. "We were a bit uncomfortable about a week ago, I said.

"I understand," said the officer with the typical calm and clear-spoken manner of the Thai people. Another officer, who was Australian and introduced himself as Mr. Keith, spoke a bit of Thai, but mostly had to ask his colleague, Mr. Poamarg to translate. He had a great sense of humor, making remarks like:

"Did you know that in Australia they eat kangaroo tail?" Nang Ya smiled, and then laughed, not laughing because of what the Australian had said, but because of the man but the way he said it. It was a relief from the stiffness of the situation, bringing a vulnerable person's mood back to a regular state. I smiled and enjoyed the treatment; in my mind they were two officers doing their job, perhaps it was part of their job to bring humor, or maybe it was just their personalities, I could not be sure. Most importantly, though, our agony was lessened and normality seemed to kick in.

Poamarg explained the refugees' situation to us, and I found this very educational: there were 40 000 people on record at the camp, where we were to be sent sometime soon. There were also about 2000 people who had just arrived and had not yet proceeded to the camp. They were in processing, having their names added to the refugee register and waiting in various police stations along the Mekong after they crossed on this side; he explained that Nang Ya and I were among these people at the moment. He went on with a serious tone.

"I would like the two of you to understand how the UN helps refugees around the world and also be aware that you are not the only ones who are going through this procedure with the UN at the moment." Nang Ya bent her head away from the officers, away from their eye contact, only peeking occasionally at me. The officer explained that at the moment there were many refugees from southern Vietnam, who were known as boat people after their plight had been picked up by international media reported that these refugees risked their lives at sea. Some drowned, or disappeared and were never discovered, but many landed in Hong Kong or the Philippines, which were crowded. The lucky ones were picked up by commercial ships; they become the UN's responsibility. Because there are too many of them, the United States has turned their back on them, so the UN must help them.

"After we get them to a safe place we find them a place to live, which takes much time and effort, not only for us, but also for volunteers around the world. The UN pays most serious attention to refugees in dangerous situations, finding them places in other countries, such as West Germany, England, Japan, Argentina and others, as quickly as possible. Western Europe took a small portion of the refugee population, but processing was slow and everyone had to wait their turn."

I turned my chair toward Nang Ya and she shifted her head upward to smile at me. I made myself more comfortable as the officer continued to speak, but wondered why he made the effort to enlighten us about the refugee problem instead of proceeding to our documentation and sending us on our way so that others might come in. To this day I don't understand why he took the time, but feel glad that he explained it to us in such a civilized way. He treated us with respect as human beings, unlike the policemen, treated us rudely and with a spirit of tyranny, without a sign of human empathy or compassion. For Nang Ya, it was a lesson which would be used in her future teaching about the plight of the refugee.

The officer went on to tell us that once our names were filed, we would receive refugee status and be protected by the United Nations. The UN rents land so that the refugees may have a temporary camp to live in while their names are on the waiting list. This list is processed in terms of how long an individual has been in the camp, and once it is your turn, you are brought for another interview. Each month, they can only take a few hundred refugees of the 40 000 who are waiting, so to find a place for everyone who is waiting will take years, he concluded. Mr. Keith gave us a copy of our application and told us not to lose it before our departure abroad. Those documents were to become our identification papers for the next three years. Mr. Keith and Mr. Poamarg then left for Bangkok, wishing us luck and shaking our hands as they went.

The hall was brightly lit, and when I looked outside, the sun had disappeared. The clock read 7. I took Nang Ya's documents and handed them to the police officer who was working the night shift, along with my own. He looked at us and said: "I have your copy. You still have to sleep in the cell, there are no rooms available." We had understood that we would no longer have to sleep in the cell, that I wouldn't have to share a room with the robbers, but it seemed that it was the only room available until our departure. During the day, however, we were free to go outside, until our 9 o'clock curfew.

We walked out of the building and went to sit on the curb. It was dark and quiet. After some time a noisy motorcycle passed by us on the street; after it had gone quite far into the distance, its engine sounded like music. This brought a pleasant feeling to me, mixed with thoughts of my past experiences of the city, nature, and my current relationship. These thoughts made me silent. Nang Ya put her arm around my back. Running alongside the sidewalk were bushy hedges, and there was nobody around to distract us. Nang Ya leaned her head against my right arm. I lifted it up and put my arm around her shoulders.

"Why does your hand always shake when I hold it?" I asked. "I don't know," she said, and told me that she was always frightened when she saw the armed policemen. Even I feared the Thai police. They were police only because of their uniforms and training, their morals were questionable at best, as they understood that in Thailand the laws were not to be reinforced, and changed according to individuals and their social standing. I was silent for a while, feeling ambivalent about the police.

When we arrived at my cell, the gate was opening, I went inside. "See you tomorrow," Nang Ya said. I nodded and watched her walk away. The gang of robbers was gone; in their place was a new couple. The husband handed me a note which read: "I was handcuffed by the police and I guess they will take me to the truck. Didn't know where you were to say goodbye. I know you are a good man, I am too. Don't let the chicken run away from the coop, ok? Your friend, the prince."

I felt relief that he was gone. I leaned my back against the wall, reading the note again. It was touching, and sending the thought of this man, this so-called prince, turning in my mind. He had some human affection, thoughts, and feelings, although his actions and personality seemed rude and unthoughtful. The man's wife asked me if I had had my supper. I smiled and told her that I had. The couple was refugees, they had been interviewed that morning, before me, but I had never seen them before. They looked kind and polite, and appeared to be educated. They slept in the corner where the gang had been, across from me and out of reach, where the wall was completely made up by the Iron Gate. People walking past in the hallway could see us; all the cells were built in that way, with only a tiny space hidden from view. The couple had piled sleeping material between us, which would block our view of each other when we were lying down. I took that tiny, hidden corner which I called a single bed, though in fact it was not a bed at all, just a piece of floor, smaller than the couple had.

When the hallway light was turned off, the room fell dark. I couldn't see anything in the room but exchanged a few words with the couple until we all fell into a deep sleep. Before I fell asleep, I kept wondering where the robbers had been taken. It wasn't any of my business, but I had lived in the same cell with them for a few days and The Prince had shared his experiences with me. The thing that struck me the most was the Prince Salaherlandsran himself. The name wasn't his real one, as his gang had told me. He had the attitude of a radical and criticized the king of Thailand, his country's most powerful man, and named himself Prince. For all those days in the cell, Prince had spoken to me regularly, but had never spoken a phrase which could be trusted, every word was made up, even the story he had told me about the woman who had borne his son lay with doubt in my mind.

I had been doing a lot of talking with my new cell-mates in the time leading up to our departure. The man told me that we were three hours north of the permanent refugee camp in Nongkhai-go. He knew the area very well; while he was a university student he used to spend his weekends in Nongkhai. He looked about thirty-five, and was tall with long hair, 60s style. He was well-spoken and spent most of his time reading while I was conversing with his wife. His wife was about twenty-eight or thirty. She had a baby-face, and was very attractive in appearance and personality. When we spoke, she often referred to her first date with her husband and we laughed when I pointed out how often she referred to him. As we spoke, I could see Mr. Satavan's eyes opening wide, with great joy, admiring his wife with deep emotion.

"Have you ever gone out with someone?" she asked. I said, without thinking, "nothing serious," and her eyes sank and she changed the subject abruptly. She and her husband insisted that we should stay in touch once we got to the camp, and told me that they hoped that we would be accepted into the same country so that we could remain friends for a long time.

The couple waited for me at every mealtime before we went down to the canteen. After I introduced them to Nang Ya, the two women immediately found all kinds of things to talk about and continued their conversation each time they met. However, Nang Ya never mentioned her two missing friends, nor did she speak of her experiences when she arrived in Thailand. I found that she was gradually becoming less distressed and laughing more. After lunch one day, we walked to the market to buy some fruit, where we found many vendors selling catfish.

There were large aluminum bowls and plastic barrels of fish everywhere. The women spent a great deal of time just looking at them, admiring them, I guess. We could not buy the fish since we had no place to cook them.

Traditionally in Thailand and Laos, women are considered to be better at fishing than men. "My mother used to buy kilos of them when I was little," Nang Ya told me. The fish seemed to be a source of inspiration for her, memories about her family were trickling out. In the fruit section there were kinds of fruit that we that we had never seen before. Dang and Nang Ya bought some of each kind and we ate them in our cells: Japanese apples as well as a variety fruits from Thailand itself.

After the lights went out in the hall, we lay down on the floor but went on talking. Nang Ya said to us, "I'd better go back to my cell now." The couple said goodnight. As she stood up to go, I pulled her arm back down. "Can you stay?" I asked. "No," she protested, pulling her arm back up, whispering that her cell-mate might wonder about her, and that Dang and her husband would think we were crazy. "The police might not let me into my cell, you know."

"I don't care what they think; I just care if you stay." I mentioned. "I can't," she said, but then went quiet and lay down beside me. When she began to cry out, I pressed my cheek against her mouth to block the sound. She pulled up her jeans in the dark and walked out of the cell. As I fell asleep, I hoped that they had let her into her cell.

CHAPTER 5

I had been doing some thinking in the past few days. The thoughts that were rustling through my mind were of how I could deal with my situation. One such thought told me I should consider Nang Ya as my life-partner. The other, however, told me that I should end our relationship before we were sent to the camp, before it was too late. If it went and, and she fell pregnant, and bore our child, that would be a reason to spend our lives together. If we were to end it now, our feelings would soon heal and we would go on to live separate lives. We had only known each other for two short weeks, had only had sex once, and it was not a good one. The night we did it, we were in the cell with the other couple sleeping over in the corner of the same room. I did not see her body and she did not see mine, we had only the sense of touch, and the experience was without climax. Long ago, when I was less than twenty years old, sex was something that made me blind, I believed it was a big deal and would cause a relationship to continue. Now I had come to realize that the relationships which hold on and last are those that are mostly in the mind, and that sex is only a portion of the relationship, and that problems should be solved before they were further complicated by more problems. One of these problems was her suspicious behaviour: her shaking and mourning and her avoidance of police officers.

The convoy of pickup trucks was lined up in front of the police station, waiting for us. Once again, I waited and was last to board the truck. I always do this, whether I am lining up for food, for an interview, for a bus; on any occasion where there is a long line-up, I am the last. I don't like crowds or competition, I find them uncivilized and embarrassing. Nang Ya had been watching me since we had met, and she put up with me without any hesitation. "You're right," she said, "There is no point in rushing." We boarded the last truck, and by the time we reached the highway, all the other trucks had disappeared from sight.

It was a calm day, from a distance the road looked as though oil had been spilled on it, shiny and black. The temperature was around thirty degrees. Nang Ya wore a blue t-shirt and I could see the tips of her nipples underneath pushing up the fabric. Her face was red, her hair was caught by the gusts of wind came through the window and floated above her ears. By the time we reached the camp in Nong khai at noon, we were feeling both excitement and fear. The camp was in the midst of flatlands that had once been rice fields. Since the government had bought the land, there were only shrubs, stretching for miles away from the camp. The buildings were made of bamboo, with grass roofs, and were laid out like the buildings in an army compound, about a hundred and fifty to two hundred feet long by fifty feet wide. Running between the buildings was a space about eight feet wide, just enough for a small pickup to pass through to deliver food and other supplies. The roads in the camp were exposed. This meant that when a pickup passed, the dust rose by the gust of wind that looking from far away like a small tornado, coating everything from the roofs to the water barrels, and turning everything it touched red.

June is the rainy season, so the dust wasn't a major concern when we arrived. Only once in while would it be a problem, until the month of November, when the monsoon rains ended. The dry season stretches from November to April, with the monsoon season beginning again in May.

There were four officers, two on each side of the entrance, with pistols at their waists. I wasn't sure if they were police officers or guards. When I saw them, they were not aggressive; they were polite and spoke to us in a well-mannered tone, so I wasn't feeling too frightened. One opened the gate to allow our truck to pass through. We drove to the end of the camp, where there were five or six buildings which were half-empty. In front of each building there were weeds growing and the ground was covered with small red rocks. Once we got out of the truck, Nang Ya and I sat on a stone beside one of the buildings, while the other couples and their children explored inside and around it.

"Are you hungry?" Nang Ya asked me. I said that I was, but that we should wait for the building officers to arrive before eating. She nodded in reply. Then I thought that I shouldn't have said that, perhaps she was hungry. "You can eat if you want," I said. She looked at me. "I'll wait." In less than a half hour, the officers arrived. One of them stood near the front of the building facing us. He looked as though he had just come from the fireplace, from the way he was sweating. He began to call our names, and when it was our turn he asked if we had any children. When I replied that we didn't, he said we should go to the building number fifty-seven, room number twenty-six. The room was at the end of the building, on the side which was furthest from the bathroom. They had assigned families with children to the rooms nearest to the water supply, which I found to be reasonable and good.

The light was dimming, so we made our bed with the tarps the aid-workers had given us, with our bags as cushions, and laid blankets over the tarps. Before eating our late lunch, Nang Ya stood in front of me and took off her jeans and her bra, leaving her blue t-shirt. She made herself at home, tearing up the magazines she had brought with her to cover the small holes in the walls which let in natural light.

"I don't like it," she said. Her long brown legs topped with their white panties caught my attention and I could not keep away from them for long. I took her hand. "What?" she asked, but at the same time her eyes closed and she dropped the piece of magazine that she had been holding. As she lay down on the tarp on her back, her t-shirt slid upward, showing her stomach. As her legs opened and we began to make love, she cried out hard this time. After a while, I lay on my back and she took my place for another few minutes. When I woke up, she was gone, saying hello to our new neighbors, as she told me when she returned.

One family a few rooms away from us had a daughter who was about eight years old who was sitting on the floor and crying. Her mother said that she missed her friends from school, and wanted to go home, and was saying that she didn't want to sleep in a buffalo house. Nang Ya sat in front of her. "I am a teacher, you know. Next week if you can find a few other students, I will teach you." The girl looked at Nang Ya, wiping away her tears and nodding her head. Her mother smiled. "When did you arrive?" she asked.

"A few hours ago." She didn't bother to introduce herself or find out their names, she was too preoccupied and didn't plan to stay in the camp for long. We at a late lunch and spent the rest of the afternoon exploring the camp.

We went to the front office to see if our names had been put on the waiting list. Inside the office, all four walls were covered with lists of names of people on the waiting list, long sheets of handwritten lists, stuck to the walls from about five feet up down to two feet from the floor. We began reading from left to right, but our names were not posted. As we left we noticed a large sheet of paper, almost as large as the portrait of the king which hung on one of the side walls. We read what was written on it; it was an official document stating the camp's regulations and dimensions. The camp was forty-five acres with a refugee population of thirty-eight thousand. All refugees must have authorized papers on them at all times as identification. Each refugee has the right to seek employment in the city with permission of the camp director and the mayor of the Noug Khai district, but the refugee must return to the camp to sleep, unless under special circumstances and with special, signed permission from the mayor.

Nang Ya was excited: this meant that she could apply for a teaching job. She took hold of my arm, squeezing it and swinging it. "You will stay in the room reading books and I will go and teach and come back every night," she said. I agreed to everything she said. We were silent for a moment, then after a short while she started talking again. "You know, if I do continue to participate and do good things for the camp, we won't stay long here, we'll be sent to the US or Canada within a year." Her temptation to work was great, but I could not know what was in her mind:

was it the money or the possibility of gaining priority on the waiting list. She looked at me with care, and curiosity about what I would say next. We passed the end of the building. There was a half of a chicken hung on our door, with a note which read: "You get a portion for today. As of tomorrow, you will have to go and wait in line for food, beginning at eight." It went on to describe what we would receive: two kilograms of rice every two weeks; fish, chicken and vegetables, and sometimes beef would be distributed each morning at the end of the building. I wondered where they were getting this valuable food for us. Nang Ya looked at me.

"I can go." I always found comfort in her exceptional personality, she always took care of any duty before I did, and if I said that I would do it, she would insist that we do it together. It was a joy to have her with me, but sometimes I would wonder about her simplicity, and whether it would eventually become heart-breaking for me. She communicated with people, never having a second opinion under any circumstances; such easy-going personality can sometimes get one into trouble, in my opinion.

We made a barbecue on hot charcoal. After our supper in the darkness, we walked to the edge of the camp. At the end of the camp was a field. Many young people hung out there, making a fire, and sometimes drinking. We were invited to join them and Nang Ya went and sat beside a girl, who then offered her a bottle wrapped in newspaper. I declined the same offer. The girl left Nang Ya sitting with the group and took my arm, pulling me with her to the field. We stood in the mist of the field in darkness and she took a cigarette from the pocket of her jeans.

"Try it," she said, "it's not a regular cigarette, and this will make you forget the past." I pushed her hand away, saying, "I don't want to forget the past, thank you anyway." She was silent, embarrassed, I guess. Later, I felt guilty about my rude behavior. "What are you doing?" Nang Ya arrived and the three of us went back together.

"You can't take him with you in the dark like that," Nang Ya said to the girl. The girl apologized, but as we returned to the circle, I saw that she was no longer talking and smiling as before, she had a sad look and seemed lost in though. I went to sit beside her and she began to cry. Nang Ya came and tapped me on the back and we walked back to our room.

Nang Ya lit the lamp and made our bed, but did not get into it, as the creaking of the bamboo floor made too much noise and would disturb the neighbors. We went outside, and with her leaning against the bamboo wall, her hands gripping the bamboo rail, we made love. She didn't want to stop and urged me to continue. I realized then that she had drunk something unusual at the fire circle. I told her to get inside and sleep. As I held her, she shook and repeated the same phrase: "I want you." Her unusual sexual behavior made me question whether it was a natural lust or desire, or whether there was something wrong with her. I did not understand her irresistible temptation. I took her to the shower and left her in there for ten minutes. When she came out she was cold, so I covered her with a towel and tried to go back to sleep. She apologized and began complaining of a headache, so I went to the neighbor to ask for an aspirin. I had no idea what had been in the drink, but resolved to never again take her to the fire circle. Besides, she was applying for a teaching job in the camp and would be busy and tired if she got it.

Chapter 6

Before her job interview, Nang Ya asked me to take a shower with her. I stood behind her, rubbing shampoo into her hair. It made a lot of lather, which dripped down her body, running down her back. The shower-head did not spray, but just ran like a tap into a sink. Once she had finished washing, we changed places; she pushed me under the tap. She washed my hair, then my back, and then she pressed her body against my back, moving her hand around to the front. I turned toward her and we made love. She seemed to enjoy it every time, and implored me to make it last longer, but afterward she would often shake and cry. This behavior made me uncomfortable; I wasn't sure what to think.

After we got dressed, we went to pick up supplies at the end of the building. People stared at her, mostly men, I guess because her outfits were very striking, although the garments themselves were simple. Before she left for her interview I asked her if she would change her clothes. I was always curious about what her intentions were in wearing such thin shirts which always seemed to fall open, but whenever I asked her about it, she asked if I wanted her to change the way she dressed. If that was the way she liked it, I had no problem with it. But since she was going for a job interview rather than going for lunch at the market, today I was more concerned. Anyway, there was no time, so I insisted that she keep the same outfit. She smiled and thanked me. I got the impression that she was not really willing to change the way she dressed, but would change if I insisted to please me. In my mind, the issue was not a big deal, and besides, she looked sexy the way she dressed. I always tried to see things from other people's perspectives. Living in the camp did not give us a real community structure, it was just a stopover, and the dress code was not really important.

By the time we arrived at the camp office, we were sweaty. Two officers were sitting behind a long table. There were white sheets of paper in front of them and both were wearing white shirts with Red Cross badges. One of the men was chewing gum and kept opening his jaw wide, as if exaggerating the movement. When he saw Nang Ya, he spat the gum out onto the dirt floor. "Which of you wants to teach?" Nang Ya said, "Me." He pushed a piece of paper toward her and gave her a pen.

"Just your full name, your room number and your refugee identity number" He told her. As she wrote, we were all silent. One of the officers went to the back room. Behind us, a crowd of people had come to check for their names on the waiting list. I heard someone screaming with excitement and joy when she saw that her name was on the departure list for the United States. Nang Ya stopped writing and turned her head to grin at the woman. The officer smiled at her and looked at his watch. She handed the sheet back to him and thanked him. "You can start teaching any time," he said, "The classes are from nine to twelve and then two to five, from Tuesday to Friday. We went back to our room and Nang Ya made lunch.

It was hot and humid, to keep ourselves cool, we would stay inside until the sun set. When night fell, Samsung, our neighbor, would often come for a visit, bringing with him a nice bottle of homemade whiskey. It was made out of rice and was white, like vodka, and very strong, probably about 40 percent. The only refuge in the camp, where people got bored and depressed waiting to have a chance at an interview, was drugs and alcohol. Simsung and his family had been living in the camp for two years, and had yet to receive any news of whether they would have the chance to go abroad. Today, after a couple of glasses of whiskey, he started to cry and talk about suicide. Nang Ya gave him a hug and he kept crying and asked me to pour him another glass of whiskey. Women hugging men was not the norm in Laos culture, Nang Ya was obviously already adapting to Western culture. After a while, he stopped sharing his bottle with us, and just drank it himself. When he emptied the bottle, he asked Nang Ya to go and get him another bottle from his wife. I wasn't a heavy drinker and was uncomfortable with his behavior. I asked Nang ya to go and see his wife, not to get another bottle, but to ask her to come and join us.

Nang Ya returned with Vone, Simsung's wife. She brought a plate of dry meat. "It's enough, Sim!" she said to her husband. He looked at her, hardly opening his eyes. "This young couple is good people, you know, I like them and they are smart too." His pointless comment irritated both of us. I understood him well enough but was not willing to go along with his self-destructive actions or accept his meaningless compliments. I shouldn't be thinking like that, I realized later, without knowing what he could be thinking. I was twenty-four years old and had been trained to follow a working-class mentality; Simsung's behavior was simply not natural to me.

As the couple went back to their room, Nang Ya remarked that the couple had a lot of experience in the social norms of our culture, meaning "men having fun when they drink and not arranging their thoughts before they speak." My sensitivity, however, could not accept Simsung's behavior. I believed that time was our teacher and that we lived our lives learning from others, who had very different sets of social and community structures and behaved accordingly. For Simsung, time passed like a river and he learned nothing from it.

As the sun went down, we took a walk. We went to a roofless hut, whose sole purpose as for cock fights. The edges of the hut were filled with spectators, not an ordinary audience, but former gamblers. Even in this camp, where everyone was waiting to leave, their addiction drove them to build this hut, and what little money they had was bet on the birds. Every single man was yelling; it seemed they wanted to encourage the roosters to fight harder, or maybe it was just out of excitement. One of the men yelled, "Fly, baby, fly!" over and over again, waving and pointing like someone losing their mind. We stood outside, and saw that when the fight ended, the money was collected. I had no idea who had won and who had lost, just that one rooster had run away, he must have been the one who lost. After the next match, one of the roosters lay dead. The owner picked it up and smashed it angrily against the rail.

"You should never have been hatched, you are really fucking chicken," he shouted. We didn't stay to watch the rooster fighting until the end, I had no interest in it, and so we went back to our building. From the building where the fighting was going on all the way back to our own, Nang Ya kept repeating the words:

"You should never have been hatched, you are really fucking chicken," and laughing to herself.

The darkness emerged. We lay on our sleeping rug but could not sleep, so we talked. For some reason, I wanted to share things about my family with Nang Ya, so I did. After my parents passed away, thirteen years ago, I always had an empty feeling, I told her. Then I had a deep relationship with a girl, and wanted to be with her for the rest of our lives, but while we were still students, she was killed by an unexploded bomb which had been buried for many years. After that, due to her death and the unlawful new political system, I changed my mind and escaped. Nang Ya was silent; I thought she was asleep, so I stopped talking.

"I am listening," she said. Her attention overcame my anxious feeling and I also wanted to hear her words, if she was in the mood to talk. But it was only when I asked her to do so, feeling as though I was the only one talking, that she reciprocated. "I wasn't meant to escape," she said, "but I am a party girl. After the communists took over, we were brought to live on-campus at the university and as you know they implemented the curfew which meant that students weren't allowed off campus after eight at night. My friends and I sometimes returned to the campus at one or two in the morning. Not only that, we were living our lives as we had under the royal government: partying, visiting friends in the village, eating food brought from our families' houses, and having boys over to our residence; all of which was forbidden by the new university regulations. That kind of lifestyle was abolished when the temporary constitution was signed in 1974. For this reason, there had been threats on my life. The rumour was that my name was on the list to be sent to a learning camp, so in fear that this would happen, I escaped."

When I asked her if she had any regrets about that time, she answered, "Not after I met you." I always believed her when she said things like this, since although she presented it as a joke; I knew that was actually how she felt. Being with her every day brought great joy to my life and I was hoping the whole thing would turn out well. "Long before the communist invasion," she continued, "during my high-school years on the weekend I used to go to the rice fields with my mother. She would bring a net and would catch basket after basket of catfish. When we brought the fish home, my uncle used to tell me that catfish eat human corpses, so for a long time I didn't eat the fish, not until I was in university. Many of my friends had told me that if I didn't eat catfish, I would die of starvation because it was the only source of food apart from rice, salt, pepper and bamboo shoots since the communists had taken over. I hope to go abroad and continue my education, to pick up where I left off. I love to teach, especially young children." She put her arm on my chest and her lips to my cheek, and the next thing I knew it was seven in the morning.

CHAPTER 7

On her first day of work, Nang Ya asked me if would come to class with her. I said I would be glad to. Since she had been told that she would be conducting the class on her own, she was a bit nervous. The school was not given a curriculum by the Thai government, but the United Nations recommended that the refugee children maintain their basic education so that when they arrived in their new countries, they would have less trouble catching up. It was also strongly recommended that the teachers give priority to English and French over other subjects. I recommended to Nang Ya that she also teach geography, especially of the Asian continent. I believe that roots are important to all human existence, and most of all for refugees. We would have to find teaching material on our own.

I sat on a bench at the back of the classroom and she began calling roll. Then, she wrote on the board what we had prepared the night before and explained it to her pupils in great detail. The classroom was full and there were three teachers in the room: Nang Ya, Miss Sorady and Mr. Suriya. Each was teaching a different subject. Nang Ya was teaching French, math and geography. The class went on with little noise from the students, each time Nang Ya raised her voice, they would go very quiet. At noon, everyone left for lunch. Shortly before class was set to resume for the afternoon session, I let Nang Ya go back to the school by herself, telling her that I would be there around three or four o'clock. After she left, I went to the main office and helped as a translator for a couple of interviews with the Australian immigration officer. By the time I reached the school it was a quarter to four.

When I reached the classroom I was dripping with sweat. Nang Ya was sitting beside the governor, Mr. Boune Narane. All the students were gone. Nang Ya came to the entrance and told me that the Thai authorities had come to congratulate the students and teachers on being a part of this school and to offer the teachers support in the form of teaching materials. The governor had appointed Nang Ya and Miss Sorady as coordinators and liaisons to the Thai authorities, until our names came up on the departures list, at which time Nang Ya would have to give up her position to another candidate. She asked me to come inside and introduced me to the officials as her boyfriend. They were all standing, waiting to shake my hand, and I did so, one by one. When it was the governor's turn to shake my hand, he just waved and gave me a dirty look. When the meeting ended, Nang Ya told me to go, saying that the governor had something to discuss with her and Sorady. I walked back with Mr. Suriya. To pass the time, I invited him into our building. Besides teaching, Suriya was a tricycle taxi driver in the camp. He was living with three young men, none of whom had girlfriends; he said that he had nothing to hurry home to after work and suggested we could go to the fire-circle if I wanted. I declined, saying that I would wait for Nang Ya. He looked at me with a sympathetic look, but did not continue his persuasion. "You can go if you like," I said.

"I will," he said, and left, adding "meet me there if you change your mind," as he stepped outside. It was half-past seven and Nang Ya still hadn't come home. I was hungry, but didn't feel like cooking. I went to Simsung's place; his wife had cooked a large pot of noodles. I told her that Nang Ya wasn't home yet and she mumbled something about Nang Ya and me, and then brought me the largest bowl. Simsung came in with a bottle of whiskey, but I told him that I had to write a letter, so I couldn't drink, but that he should go ahead. As he took out a glass, his neighbor came into the room.

"I saw the light," he said. Simsung introduced me to the neighbor, but I have since forgotten his name. The three of us sat in the room, which was about the size of a chicken coop, and the neighbor told us that there was a kid who had hanged himself on a branch near the fire-circle. Simsung's wife asked him if it was true that many kids and adults had committed suicide in the camp before they had arrived, and if anyone was aware of it and if things were being done to prevent it from happening. The neighbor said, "This is a refugee camp," called sero in Lao. Things happened and then passed, and we shouldn't take anything into consideration apart from our own problems, he said. "It is nothing, people are not connected."

I excused myself and left. I went to our room, and saw that it was already nine o'clock. Not long after, Nang Ya came in, smelling of alcohol and cigarettes and something else I could not identify. "Sorry, the governor took us out to the restaurant in the town. He offered for me to teach math in an elementary school in Nongkhai which would pay all my expenses: a taxi, meals and clothing."

"Are you going to take the offer?" I asked. "I don't know yet, I needed to talk to you first. I'll be back in a few minutes,

I'm going to take a shower," she said. When she returned, she did not ask what I had eaten for supper, but continued telling me how gentle and kind the governor had been. I told her what I had eaten and that I had been to Simsung's place. "They are good people," she said.

Nang Ya put on her long t-shirt as usual before she came to bed. As she laid her back down, I put my arm across her stomach, about to pull up her t-shirt, but she stopped my hand. "Sorry, I'm tired." I turned my back to her and we slept until morning. When I woke up, I was in a strange mood. I was wondering why Suriya hadn't been invited for supper at the restaurant. He had been teaching for more than three months. And why had Nang Ya changed her attitude: she used to be the one who initiated and enjoyed lovemaking, and was always creating the mood by telling romantic stories or wearing striking outfits. Then I though, things could be worse, I should not intervene in her situation, whatever it might be. Besides, this was a camp; a relationship with someone was like renting a home without a contract.

From the first day Nang Ya started teaching, Suriya was always stopping by our place to chat. One day he sat down beside the door and asked me: "Did you hear about the Jim Jones mass suicide on Bangkok post last week?" The next day, he brought me a magazine so that I could read about it. Later on that year, with the savings he had from taxiing people around the camp, he bought a Sony radio. "You keep the radio with you, ok?" he said, "So you can listen to what is going on around the world." Suriya and I were becoming good friends. He seemed to see things and translate them while I was just seeing them in an innocent way, trusting them although they were filled with hints to their meaning. He did not simply tell me about the events of the world, he added in very detailed information, which was often depressing. The disturbances on the Chinese and Vietnamese borders which I read about in the Bangkok Post were horrifying.

On the third Friday of Nang Ya's teaching job, she slept over in Nongkhai. For no reason I could see, I was very depressed that night. Suriya came over in the morning before class, bringing me a coffee and sitting with me for a while, until Nang Ya arrived. She was well-prepared and dressed professionally. She had a book with her, a biography of Amvar Sadath. She stayed with me for a while and chatted before class. Her boss, whose name she did not mention, though I could only think that it must be the governor; had rented a place for her, a nice one-room apartment, and had given her all the equipment she needed to do her job. She would still need to come to the camp once in a while to maintain her refugee status, so that the camp administration would leave her name on the refugee waiting list. We had been living together for three and a half months as a couple; I had become much attached to her. Given her unknown situation, living in town, and supported by a powerful man, the governor, I lived in uncertainty, fear, worry, depression and anxiety. Waking up without seeing her, going to bed without the hope that she would come, and seeing her for only a short time each day were strange. On a daily basis, I wondered what had gone wrong with me, and if everyone had similar experiences.

On that unpleasant day, I went to the whiskey-stand. At that moment I was out of my space. The man tending the stand poured me some straight whiskey. "I know," he said. I wasn't sure what he knew. There were many things that a person could be depressed about: living in the camp too long, loved ones disappearing or escaping, or something else, I wasn't sure if he knew my situation. I drank, but stared at pedestrians and tricycles passing each other in both directions on the dusty temporary street. There was nothing to cheer you up in the camp other than someone you loved, and who you maybe hoped to start a family with. There was nothing here in the moment to be happy about, but at least there could be someone who cared about you. My thoughts dripped away easily, everything here was short, with no expanse, and there was nothing to drive you! Was that what the man was talking about when he said he knew?

"If I had a phone, I would call Jimmy Carter to get me out of here," the bartender said, and laughed. He looked calm, and was always smiling and talking to his customers as though he had known them all his life. My hope of getting an interview and getting out of the camp was slim without Nang Ya's presence. Suriya finished work and joined me at the stand. We drank. "Did you ever get so drunk that your head was spinning and someone had to take you home and you missed school the next day and you failed the course and your frinds said you were a good guy but stupid?" Suriya asked, laughing at his nonsense remarks.

"What is the point of you bringing that up?" I asked. "My point," he continued, "is no point. Whiskey gives you a point!" We left the stand, hanging on to one another to get to Simsung's room. Suriya banged on his door, and he shouted to us that he would be out in minute. More than ten minutes later, he still hadn't come out. Suriya said, "He must be finishing what he is doing." We waited, and he came out wearing a pair of shorts, asking what we wanted.

"We are going to the fire circle, are you coming with us?" We went to the fire circle and we each danced with a girl. The girl who had taken me to the field was there, and she asked where Nang Ya was. "She is working."

"Oh, a job in the camp, that is a surprise!" she said. I danced with the girl, song after song, and she said "I don't have a boyfriend, I don't want to, but I want to make out with different boys." It was at this moment that I realized that our culture and customs no longer existed in this camp; we were living free from our beliefs. Our lives here were nothing more than our animal instincts, nobody thought before they acted or spoke. Everything happened out of control. If you wanted to have sex with someone, you just asked for it, only the older people showed any control over the temptation. We no longer had any belief system.

Suriya was still dancing with the same girl he had started with. First they danced around the fire like the other couples, then moved away from the fire and disappeared. Simsung was just sitting and talking to an older girl, he looked delighted, but never got up to dance. Of course, he was a married man, he wasn't here looking for fun with the girls, drinking and smoking were his main interests. After Suriya had been gone for a few minutes, I was feeling a bit worried, and found myself thinking about Nang Ya and what she had been doing in the town with the politician. I wanted to mention this to Suriya or Simsung, but they were both occupied. The girl, without speaking, took my arm and started dancing ahead of me. I danced along with her. "There is no point in being sad," she shouted, "life is too short. Besides, there is no future to think about, just live your life!" She took hold of my hand and pulled me down to sit.

"I saw your girlfriend the last time, she seemed like a very jealous person, maybe she loves you too much," the girl said. I nodded. "What happened?" she asked. "I don't think you should know."

"Okay, thanks for your concern, though," I said. "Any time. You don't have to date me, you know, we can just be friends.

Any time you need to talk, just let me know, okay?" She was not much older than I was, so how could she be so calm and kind? She made very direct remarks about everything, even sex. However, I could not detach myself from my uncivilized male ego. Despite her calmness, she had many friends who came to her with their problems and asked her to read their palms. She could tell who would live and who would die and of what cause, which all seemed ridiculous to me. She was good-looking, but for some reason I had no desire to find out her life story.

Suriya returned from the darkness. The girl he had been dancing with had gone home, so he and I continued drinking, but not talking to each other. The night breeze came and we all stretched our arms behind our backs and looked up at the skies. They were dark, but were filling with stars that looked like lanterns seen from a distance. As we ignored the dancing and turned our attention to deep conversation, the girls began to leave for home. A couple of boys were still there, but they too were preparing to leave, putting their cassettes and radio into bags. "See you guys later!" they called as they walked away from the circle, their singing disappearing into the distance. As I stood up to say goodbye to the girl, she put her hands on my cheeks and started kissing me. I pulled away. "I like you, you are a very attractive soul, but like you say, my girlfriend in jealous. See you!"

On our way back to the building, Simsung asked us not to take him to the circle again. I respected his decision; he was married with two children and was worried that he would be sent back to Laos. He had no formal education, no proof that he would be able to adapt to life abroad. His wife did not have the requirements either, so their chance of getting an interview was slim. It was a matter of fact, something we all worried about; all refugees were caught in the same category. First our names were on the list for refugee status, then second was the interview, then the acceptance list, then finally the departure list. Each waiting list could take six months to five years, until the end of the contract between the UN and the Thai government for this seventy-acre refugee camp which held forty-five thousand refugees. Before we parted ways, we apologized to Simsung, with Suriya saying, "We can still be friends, right?" Simsung said: "I didn't mean we had to break our friendship!" I felt once again like a child, talking to a friend this way. I thought of going back to my room and sleeping for twelve hours straight.

When I entered the room, I heard the floor squeak. I lit the kerosene lamp, and Nang Ya was there. She sat up, stretched her arms out and held me tight. "I miss you Bo." She pushed me down onto the bed on my back and positioned herself on top of me. It had been over a week since we had had sex, and given the unknown circumstances of her stays in town, I was less tempted by her sexually than usual. I was more concerned with the demise of our relationship. Nang Ya was very sexually active, and I wondered if her sense of morality was on a normal level, if she was capable of understanding her own pride and dignity, or if she ignored them. The stakes were high in the camp, one had no goal in life (except for getting out of the camp), and it seemed to be a test from the universe, a test to see who will succeed and who will drown. Was it worthwhile for me to convince Nang Ya to reduce her drive and temptation for money and material things? Or should I let her be and concentrate on my own future, occupying myself with helping others who needed some activity until their departure date. What about my love for and attachment to her? Did it count, and was it worth the effort to bring her back? These thoughts were running through my mind as I lay on the floor, and I did not make any moves to show that she was tempting me. All the same, I felt it was best that I had not brought the girl home with me.

I had no problem getting up at the usual time. Suriya was shouting outside the door, "Come to class, you might have a chance to see Nang Ya!" He left for class. Nang Ya turned to me and smiled. "Did you miss me?" she asked, and held me close. "I don't just miss you, I love you," I said. I saw a tear run down her cheek, but did not say anything. "I'm sorry for leaving you alone." She put on her jeans and went out in bare feet to get us Oval tine. After she left for class I read until noon.

Nang Ya said that she was free for the next couple of weeks and that she would spend time with me. I proposed that next weekend she could bring me to see where she worked in town. She didn't look happy about this, but agreed to take me there, saying that we could go to a matinee at the movies after. Nang Ya knew the people at the camp's gate, so getting me a pass was no problem, and getting a taxi would also be easy. Late that afternoon, Suriya walked back from school with Nang Ya. He stopped to chat with me for a few minutes and said that Nang Ya had told him that I was going to visit her work in town. When he asked when we were going, I pointed to Nang Ya.

"This coming Saturday," she said. He nodded and said: "That is good for him." I could see that Suriya had been observing my mood since Nang Ya took the teaching job. Her work took an enormous amount of time, and most days she would stay in town, in the apartment that the governor had supplied her, which caused curiosity and various imagined scenarios in my mind. I guessed that they had been talking about this at school, perhaps with Sorady as well, but I didn't know her as well, she always rushed home after work. I heard that her boyfriend's parents were drowned while swimming across the Mekong. This family tragedy created a lot of grief in surviving members. Sorady was a sweet woman of twenty-four. She had completed her teaching degree a year before her escape. She and her boyfriend had no desire to apply to go to the United States or Canada; they only wanted to go to France, that's where most of their relatives were. They had been there permanently since 1975, after the communists took over Laos. The sun was setting, around it was all red. The narrow path from our building to the main street was dusty, and there were people throwing water on the ground, trying to keep the dust from rising. Suriya jumped from time to time to keep from stepping on wet ground, but Nang Ya and I ignored it and carried on. The moment he disappeared from our sight, we went inside and started cooking. Nang Ya wasn't in her usual talkative mood, she was avoiding my comments altogether. She mostly said "yes" and nodded absently. I felt she must be feeling irritated with me, so I stopped talked and tried to just be quiet. After we finished cooking and began to eat, she started sobbing. I asked her what was wrong and if she would tell me about it. She looked straight at me and shook her head. I did not speak anymore, just stroked her cheek and kept eating until I had finished. Since she wasn't going to tell me what she was feeling, I left her free to contemplate, leaving the building and wandering around the camp with no destination in mind.

After a while, I thought about the girl I met at the fire-circle, and how once she had said I was strange. I didn't normally try to convince anyone of anything, especially women. Whenever someone showed signs of not enjoying my company, I tended to distance myself and believe that they didn't appreciate my presence. However, the girl had told me that women in general needed persuasion, and that a man should take more time to figure out the real feelings of the other. In terms of my personality, I didn't like it when people put pressure on me, or anyone else. In spite of this, the girl might speak something of the truth on that matter. Nang Ya might need to tell me something, but was delaying telling me so that she could see whether I would accept the situation that I hadn't been aware of.

I went back to the building. I sat down in our room and she came up behind me and pressed my body against her front. I could hear her breathing, and feel her breasts against my back. "I am sorry, Bo, I don't mean to keep anything from you, but there is something I cannot tell. In the beginning, the governor said that I would teach math in town, and then said that I would not be doing any teaching, working instead as a coordinator. Now I am doing more of that work, and was asked to stay in town permanently. I don't want you to be surprised about my apartment in town; we can spend the night there if you like. It is actually more of a bungalow than an apartment."

"Alright," I answered, pulling her around to face me, "You don't have to worry about anything about me. Whatever you do, I will go along." She looked me in the eyes, searching. "Don't you want to know what I have been doing?" she asked. "I want to know everything you do without me, but I won't force you to tell me. I would appreciate it if you would tell me, but you don't have to if you don't want to. You can cancel our date if you want."

I had always thought that jealousy made one angry. I had never found myself in an angry moment, anger wastes energy and loses friends. If I was going to lose friends, it was going to be without an angry approach. I would have liked to say to Nang Ya that she shouldn't get involved with any kind of activity in Thailand in general. We were living in the camp temporarily, waiting to be called. I knew, however, that if I said what I was thinking, she would agree, since that was her nature, but that it would never be a decision that she really accepted. I saw that she would never have the freedom to fulfill her own desires, and I often felt guilty about that. I didn't have the courage to challenge her about it, but I wished she would be satisfied to be with me forever.

If there is any secret that one person wants to keep from the other, there should not be pressure to be told. Forcing out a secret like that is immoral, I would rather be sad from the other one being unwilling to tell me than get the truth that way. We went to town as planned on Saturday. As soon as we came out of the taxi and I saw the style of the bungalow, my heartbeat increased. The whole street looked similar, small bungalows of the same size. At the front there were iron gates painted black, about three feet high. There were flowers and bushes scattered around, about six feet apart. All the buildings were white. Nang Ya opened the door and directed me to go in. The kitchen and the living room were in the same section, right at the entrance. After dropping her bag on the table, looking excited, she took my arm and led me to the bedroom behind the kitchen. There was no door between the two rooms, or rather three rooms, counting the living room. The bed was queen-sized, with large pillows and clean sheets. Nang Ya released my arm and excused herself to the bathroom. I had expected that the room would be for working, as she had told me, with a desk and other office equipment, but there was none. I admired the apparent comfort of the bed and the furniture. I looked out the window, it was quiet outside, and there were no pedestrians, just tuke-tukes passing by in both directions. Nang Ya came out of the bathroom wearing a brown robe. She sat beside me, leaning her head on my shoulder.

"I wish we had a room like this in the camp. Don't you think?" she asked. I turned toward her and kissed her deeply. She stood up to undress me and then slid her back up the bed, taking her robe off and tossing it on the floor. As soon as I turned to her, placing my body on top of hers, she hooked her legs behind me and drew me closer. Her thighs tightened against me and I felt the joy and desire as never before. Afterward, I went to the bathroom. I found her miniskirt, underwear, shoes and everything on the floor beside the toilet bowl. Behind the mirror, there was a small shelf on which there was an old cookie box, which turned out to be filled with condoms. Seeing it, my heart sank, my ears burned and I broke down. I closed the mirror and sat down on the closed toilet.

"Are you ok?" she asked. "Just a minute!" I shouted back. I stepped into the shower stall and turned on the water. I stood there with my head under the shower to cool myself. Nang Ya stepped in and we took a shower together.

We got out of the shower together and Nang Ya dressed in the bathroom while I went back to the bedroom. I had a headache and no longer wanted to see the movie. She came out after she had fixed herself up, looking as though she knew that something had gone wrong. I told myself that I should leave, and if she wanted to stay, that was fine with me. She stared into my eyes seriously and saw my tears begin to drip. She went into the bathroom and started to sob as well. I went in and told her that I would wait for her outside. She reached out to me, nodding.

For the thirty minutes in the taxi, neither of us had any words. As soon as I arrived, I went to our room and changed my jeans for shorts, a t-shirt and sandals, and walked to Suriya's place. One of his roommates opened the door. "He's at the soccer field coaching kids," he told me. I went to the field and watched the game. Suriya saw me, but was too busy to come over, he must have thought that whatever I wanted to share with him wasn't so important that it couldn't wait until the end of the match. After, he walked up to me. "Wait until you've heard what I have to say before you take a shower," I said. "Ok," he said, lifting his shirt to wipe the sweat from his face, "what is it?"

We went to the outskirts of the camp, and sat together on a large pile of lumber, our feet dangling a few inches from the ground. The grassy ground was stacked with dried cattle manure. Suriya remarked that in some countries, they used the dried manure in place of firewood. I wasn't interested in his remark, and waited for him to shut up, but he did not. "I thought you and Nang Ya had a date today?" he said.

"That is why I came to see you." The expression in his eyes and on his face became anxious. I explained what I had found in Nang Ya's apartment and what had happened. I asked him what he knew about the situation, and the governor's proposal to Nang Ya and Sorady. Only then did he lean his shoulder against mine and tell me about the offer that the governor had made the first day he offered Nang Ya and Sorady the teaching position.

The day the governor had come to the camp to inspect the school; he had no intention of supporting the venture or supplying them with materials. The Thai government was not supplying a budget for education in the camp; it was not part of protocol. It was standard for the school to be set up by someone in the camp, a refugee, perhaps with recommendations from a non-profit organization. The teacher taught out of their own charity, and to encourage them, the camp directors would sometimes bring them small tokens, like food or supplies for other daily needs. I knew this already, as sometimes Nang Ya had brought such things home with her. However, the governor offered Nang Ya and Sorady three hundred Baht each per month, separate from the school, just for his own fulfillment. Sorady took the offer right away, and Nang Ya agreed shortly after.

"As she told me later," he said, "she did not understand his plan for her teaching then, she said that sometimes she thought that he wanted her to teach his own children math and French." Suriya was silent for a while. He looked at my eyes and continued talking. "You can hit me if you like," he said, "but Nang Ya took the offer for several reasons. She needed the three hundred to send home to her disabled mother, who is alone since Nang Ya's father was arrested and sent to the learning camp. She loves you, Bo she is always talking about your humor and how much fun you are to be with. She wanted for this year to be over so she could spend the rest of her life with you. I think the governor also threatened her. Sorady didn't want to have a close relationship with you and Nang Ya, for fear that if everything were exposed you would blame her. So, that is the situation. It's not usual, but we've all come across unexpected experiences here in the camp. The reason Nang Ya was willing to take you to the apartment is because the governor is attending a conference in Bangkok for two weeks. Nang Ya wanted you to enjoy her cosy temporary room; she said that since you two met, you've never had the opportunity to sleep in a real bed instead of on a rug on a dirt floor.

I was flexing my arm and slid down off the lumber. I started to walk away. "I'm sorry I had to tell you," Suriya said. I realized it had taken him a long time to bring up Nang Ya's relationship with the governor, the fifty-five year old tyrant. He suggested that I should talk to Nang Ya and try to make it up and ask her to end the relationship with the governor, to put the past behind us. I found his suggestion reasonable, but boring. I didn't feel like making an effort to speak to her on any subject, or even start a conversation. I wished that the whole situation had never happened, that I had never started questioning her during our waiting period at the police station months ago.

I admired Suriya for his appraisal of the situation. He was about three years older than I was, well educated, and lived his life approaching every situation and occurrence with reason. Above all, he was free from romantic involvement and emotional downturns. He was good-looking, and building a loving relationship with a woman would likely have taken little effort on his part, but he had taken the decision not to at this time. I found myself trapped in emotional disaster from painful experiences, one after another, and seemed o have little capacity to avoid them.

When we got back to the building, he insisted on staying with us for a little while. While Nang Ya prepared supper, we went to have a shower. I lent him one of my towels. I told him I was angry about the matter, but didn't know how to solve it. After showering, we stood at the entrance. It was late, and not many men were going in and out of the building. Suriya told me that anger was not in my nature, and that it was inappropriate for cultured men such as us to show it, so I should let it seep away by itself. I didn't think I could take his advice, but his approval brought tranquility to my mind. I had always been that way; getting approval from someone always enhanced my self-esteem. After we had eaten, he went home.

I thought again about my state of mind, and the fact that everyone has the power to select their own path when being provoked by external aggression. Anger has no logic, it is a short strike of thoughts when our ego pushes them up, and the aggressive actions which result are not good. Nang Ya wasn't in the mood to wear one of her striking sleeping outfits. She wore a long t-shirt, which slid up above her thighs when she lay down. I found her attractive, but wasn't in the mood to touch her. The anger in my mind wasn't shown in my external appearance, but it still affected my state of mind and reduced my desire. She turned her back against mine as we slept. I began having a terrible dream: the governor, who I had only met the one time, in the classroom, came into our bedroom and cut off my arm with a sword. I saw three men wearing black outfits like divers;

the tallest of the three called himself a king, and ordered the other two to guard the entrance. The tall one took my feet in one hand and I saw that in his other hand he held a long and sharp sword, and he quickly dropped one blow on my arm. I saw my arm fall off, dropping to lie beside my body, with blood spilling everywhere. I called to Nang Ya for help, but she had disappeared, gone into the mists of the field. I screamed, and then I felt a heavy object on my chest, almost cutting off my breath. I awoke, and Nang Ya had laid her head on my chest with her arms around my body, and was shaking me awake. I looked at her for a moment and thanked her. In the dark I could only feel her presence, and could not know of her emotional state.

Communication between us seemed to be out of reach. I went back to sleep and sometime later felt the blankets shaking. I turned to face her back and put my arm over her. I realized that she had been crying in her sleep. I shook her awake and held her against me. She began to cry more loudly and talking at the same time. "I never meant to hurt you, I just needed the money, and I was stupid." She went on and on as I held her. She said that she had never felt as close to any man before in her life as she felt to me. I turned to face her, with my chin above her forehead, and we slept through until morning.

Chapter 8

Suriya had been doing a lot of thinking about us, he told me later. One late afternoon after school, he took me to meet Mr. Yee. My first experience of this man was nearly walking into the path of his spitting. He chewed tobacco and spat constantly without checking to see if there was anyone in the way. He was no more than five feet tall, and had a shaved head like a retired monk. He spoke very quickly, without making eye-contact, and was always occupied with something else as he spoke. I found him annoying and found his attitude rather distracting, but Suriya had been telling me what a good man he was, that he was honorable and would say what he meant and do what he said; he was impressive in many ways. Knowing myself, and knowing that I also had a disagreeable attitude, I immediately thought we would get along well.

Mr. Yee ran a small tricycle taxi company in the camp. He owned eighteen tricycles and rented them for twenty baht a day. Suriya rented one of them and made about thirty to fifty baht a day. The profit was appealing, if I could make as much as Suriya, Nang Ya could have enough money to send to her mother each month, and she wouldn't need to do what she had been doing anymore. Then we could live in the camp and be together every day until our departure from the camp. There was nothing that could compare to my feelings after Suriya found this job for me. I wrote down my name and address for Mr. Yee and left a five baht deposit. He said I could come and get the tricycle whenever I wanted the next morning, "As long as it is after six!" he shouted after me. The rental was from six in the morning to six at night, and there was no reduction in rent if you took it for fewer hours than the full day.

I went back to my room feeling very excited. Suriya had left for a soccer match. Nang Ya came out to greet me with a faint smile; but soon she was as excited as I was that I should have a job driving a tricycle taxi. She was preparing supper as usual, but didn't have much to say about my new job. Deep down in her mind, though I didn't know and couldn't be sure, she seemed frightened. The veins in her throat were standing out and ticking and look on her face was that of someone who was going through trauma or the death of someone close to them. However, she didn't speak of her feelings, just looked at me sympathetically.

"Good, Suriya is a good guy, I like him," was all she said. I thought maybe she was concerned about my ability to do the job, it didn't occur to me that she might fear that the governor would do me harm since I had asked her to put an end to the affair. My taking this job was one of the preparations we were taking so that she could tell him that she wouldn't see him anymore. I was so naïve about Nang Ya's role in town. I never thought about blackmail or threats from someone in a high-ranking position, not believing that anyone could do something so terrible.

The darkness arrived. I felt very emotional about the ordeal of the past few days and was looking forward to a long session of lovemaking that evening. But when I proposed this to her, she simply lay on her back on the rug and lifted her shirt and opened her legs, with no participation. Afterward I was silent, but she was tossing and turning. The next morning she told Suriya that she was quitting teaching, so he took me with him instead to replace her. I hesitated, saying that I would still have to pay the rent for the tricycle, but Suriya said it was no big deal, that we could taxi for three hours after school to pay for the rent. He said that those were the hours when the vendors were closing their stands, so everyone had a lot of things to carry home and would pay extra.

The vendors were those who had come to the camp with some capital who ran businesses to keep their money from depleting as they waited to leave. Suriya called these people long-term festival sellers. The students were curious about me becoming their teacher. I spent the first thirty minutes explaining who I was and that I would be replacing Nang Ya. One thirteen-year-old girl spoke out: "I know who you are!" When I answered jokingly, "Well, that's scary!" the students all laughed. The girl explained over the laughter that I was Nang Ya's boyfriend, and that Nang Ya had shared her secret thoughts with her, saying that after the two of us went abroad, we would get married and have four children. The children were staring at the girl, most of them smiling. I saw that all this discussion was a waste of time, so I started teaching.

Since I had been doing the lesson plans with Nang Ya, I fell easily into teaching them a history lesson on Laos and Thailand, and the connection between the two countries, being careful to point out that almost a third of Thai people spoke Lao. They showed great interest in all this and were very cheerful. At the end of the day, I told them that I might come back, and the girl who had spoken earlier asked if she could visit Nang Ya at home if she wasn't going to be coming back to school. I told her that it wouldn't be a problem; she could come anytime she was invited. It struck me afterward that I had given my students a detailed history lesson, but they were all around ten years old; I should have taught them only basic language and math. However, there was no curriculum to follow.

A week later, I had raised seven hundred baht. The money was more than enough for Nang Ya to send to her mother in Laos. It would cover her medical bills and household expenses. She said that she had to go to town and that the governor would return from Bangkok any day now. I sat in front of the door with my chin in my hand.

"Do you love him?" I asked. She looked at me with strange eyes, and almost yelled: "I don't know!" He was old enough to be her father. Since they had met he had always offered her something: taking her for a short trip, eating at a restaurant, going shopping, going to the movie theatre, and sometimes watching pornography at a hotel. These activities left many questions I wanted to ask, but she still could not say whether she loved him or not. Every time he sent someone to pick her up, she had no will of her own to say no, but simply went along with him until whatever amount of time he had to spend with her was over, at which time he told her he was no longer available. She said she felt no disappointment at that time, it was then that she came back to be with me. There is an old saying that when one has no mind of one's own; it is like being held as an anaconda's ghost. One did not notice until it had swallowed your entire body, and there were only seconds left before your heart stopped beating.

In my mind, I never intended to allow her to go and see the governor. But, when she told me that she was going to go and see him, I did not have any more will than she did to resist. She had been lying to me for a long time up before I found her out on the day that we went to her temporary home. I had been saying before when she told me she was working in town, I expected her home to be filled with office equipment, but as it turned out the house was no more than a high-class brothel; nothing she had told me was true.

There were no words to describe what this had done to be, and yet I still felt tied to her by the circumstances we were in. If we had been living a normal life, I could have walked away easily, but here, since our names were listed together, as a couple, on the waiting list, separating from her would be like a death sentence. The camp could be closed down any time, whenever the UN stopped sending supplies.

She picked up her small things and walked off, saying nothing more than "I'll love you always" as she went After she disappeared, I thought that she was no longer herself, but an anaconda, a ghost, a ghost that had sucked out her spirit. Now she was no more than a sleepwalker. As the sun rose, the hot air began to rise with it. I went inside to change my clothes, and a moment later Suriya was banging on the door.

"I dropped Nang Ya off at the front gate, let's go," he said. We went to the school and I began teaching. During second period, the camp administration team arrived with the camp director, Mr. Boane Yang. He proposed a short meeting, so we sent the children outside. Some began running and chasing each other. Hearing the increasing disorder outside, the director said he would hire more teachers. There were two teachers there with him already, and he would need four more, to make six teachers in total. Suriya and Sorady would remain as senior teachers, so one new teacher would replace Nang Ya and the rest would make it possible to have smaller groups of children and a more orderly school. Since I hadn't signed my name on the teacher list, I wasn't mentioned as part of the teaching team, but after the meeting the director asked if I would consider participating for the benefit of the children. I quickly declined, but afterward felt guilty about rejecting the offer. He did not wait for an explanation, but simply thanked me for filling in for Nang Ya for a couple of days. Before we left, Suriya said, "Now you can taxi all day." He gave me a pat on the back and we left. Feelings were always unpredictable, and I felt thankful that the universe sent me things to stimulate my mind and look forward to the days to come.

I ate lunch alone at the stand closest to the front of the camp. I watched the gate opening and closing, imagining that at any minute someone would come to drop off Nang Ya, and that she would run to me and hug me and that we would go back to our room and make love all day. A police car drove in, with two officers in it. One stayed in the car; the other stepped out on the passenger side. He went to the guard's booth and spoke to the man inside for a couple of minutes before coming out with a large envelope in his hand. He went back to the car and it drove off, heading further into the camp. About forty minutes later, when I was inside the main office, I saw the car pass again. Now there was a man in the backseat wearing handcuffs. I got back on my tricycle and headed back to the market. I wondered who it had been in the back of the car. This sort of arrest was a daily occurrence; I had heard of them often, but hadn't seen one until this time.

That afternoon, the sun burnt most of my body; my arms, legs and face had all changed color. When I arrived at the market, Vana, one of my regular customers, said: "You look great, Bo, with black skin!" When I took off my sunglasses, she laughed and said that I looked like a raccoon. She told me to park my taxi behind the stand and asked if I could give her a hand with her stand. We stacked two more tables with the one that was already there to give her more space. Vana placed a basket of live chickens on the floor under the tables. In her stand she sold all kinds of vegetables along with the chickens. She gave me seven baht for my help and that was a good profit.

Vana was in her late forties with a good sense of humor, which is what caught my attention. In the late afternoon, I went to pick her up. When we arrived at her place, her husband, who was a mobile barber, helped us to unload the unsold items. I cleaned up the tricycle a bit before I brought it back to Mr. Yee, As I was leaving, Vana called after me: "Come and have supper with us, go and get Nang Ya first, if you'd like." I nodded my head and left. By the time I returned, the darkness had emerged. I was uncomfortable about telling her that Nang Ya had left me, and that I didn't know if she would return to me this time, and that she had quit her teaching job. Vana's husband was lighting the lamp as I entered."The sun was very bad today, huh?"

"Yes, it was!" I replied. Vana asked about Nang Ya. I told her what had happened, without mentioning the affair with the governor. Vana looked worried and said that I should go to see the monk. She said that she didn't believe that I had a fox's attitude, always looking to steal and kill. I thanked her for her concern and her compliment to my character, and said that it wasn't so bad. I had a few friends who I could still get in touch with and talk to occasionally. After supper, Vana's husband handed me a cigarette and lit one for him.

"I don't smoke," I said. He patted the pack on the kerosene barrel sitting beside him and said that if I didn't smoke, I shouldn't start. He asked what I was doing with myself. I told him that I rose early each morning and jogged for an hour before starting work. I told him that I met many people in my new line of work. He said it was a good thing and told me that I was welcome any time in his home.

My room was dark, and when I lit the lamp I saw Nang Ya's notebook. I opened it and began to read. On the first few pages she had written her teaching schedule, which was followed by some notes on cooking and the things I liked to eat: "Bo likes seafood." After this comment, there was a long paragraph which she seemed to have written to be funny: "We don't have luxury food, my love, but I can cook you food that is even better than seafood." I read this with enjoyment, this note was an expression of a private joke meant for her, speaking about me and how she cared for me. I could still not fathom how she could leave me for the governor, who was as old as her father. Something really frightening must have happened for her to leave me.

My jealousy quickly led to anger this time. The nights I had spent alone had tortured me. There was silence, the sounds of the night were nothing more than the crickets chirping, the sound of them was everywhere, but they were nowhere to be seen. I woke up in the middle of the night and wandered along the dusty streets to the end of the camp, and by the time I got back to our building it was dawn. Just as I laid my head down, Suriya banged on the door. I woke up and walked over to let him in. "You look like a charcoal salesman," he said, "what's wrong? "I didn't sleep last night." He told me that I had to let it go, and asked me to come jogging with him. I said that I needed to get some rest before the sun rose. "You have to respect your customers," he said, "or they will find another taxi!" He left and started running, and I went back to sleep.

Chapter 9

I had been working many hours throughout the week. Simsung dropped in once early in the week to tell me that his family had been called up for an interview with the US immigration officers. I congratulated him and wished him well on passing the questionnaire. He thanked me, smiling with joy, and said that he would tell me all about it later. After he left, I thought about him for a while, he didn't seem to understand the refugee situation, and instead he panicked about unrelated things he imagined, and then showed visible relief when they did not come to pass. I hoped that the translator was helpful in pointing him in the right direction with the questioning, so that he would not be disappointed again.

That Sunday, Suriya came to ask if I wanted to go fishing. In the camp, there was no such thing as a weekend, but for the school-children and Suriya, as their teacher, Sunday was a day off. He gave me a pass for the front gate, and I went to ask Mr. Yee if I could borrow the tricycle. "I've told you many times," he said, "You don't have to borrow it as long as you pay me."

"You've missed my point," I said, "I'm saying that I will take the tricycle to go fishing, and if I catch any fish I will give you some." He scratched his head for a moment and then said, "Ok, take it; you kids are complicating my thoughts." Suriya winked at me and told me to hurry up before Mr. Yee changed his mind. I told Suriya about Simsung's family being called up for an interview. Suriya was glad, and said "I hope he makes it!" I told him that I hadn't seen Simsung since. We decided that we would bring him some fish that night. When we got to the river, or rather the creek, it couldn't really be called a river as it was less than ten feet wide; we set ourselves up on the bank. Most of the fish we caught were catfish, and they were larger than the ones we had in Laos, with more meat. We met many fishermen and women there, since those who arrived early at the creek caught baskets full of fish. Since we had arrived later, we caught less than fifty of them between the two of us. The creek was a few miles from the camp, with black rocks and trees lining the banks. It was nice and shady, though, and was out of the sun all day. I had a feeling of great calm, sitting on the bank and watching the others fish.

Suriya's two friends brought their girlfriends with them. One girl was deaf, but was very pretty, and had a kind manner. She and the other girl prepared us lunch, she was wearing tight jeans and white t-shirt; I had trouble not thinking of Nang Ya. I wished she were there, we would have had fun, and I found myself thinking about the stories she had tome about catfish. One in a while, the girl brought us drinks and fried bananas, smiling all the while. The heat made us sweaty, the girls were all dripping. Once in a while, one of them would roll up her jeans and dip her feet into the water, watching us fishing. Each time one of us caught something, one of the girls would race to get a pail to put the fish in. We continued fishing until the sun was halfway to the horizon, and then packed up our things and left. Suriya told me I would have to go quickly so that the fish would not go bad and begin to smell. This seemed like him looking for a reason to boss me around. We took turns pedaling, changing places frequently. When we arrived at the gate, the guard asked to be paid, saying that the passes we had were only good for four hours. He said we were late by two hours, and to avoid trouble, we paid him fifteen baht each.

"Cheap corruptor," said one of the girls once we had passed. "Why did you say that to him?" the other girl exclaimed. They began exchanging remarks about the guard and accusing one another or flirting with him, which carried on until we reached Suriya's place. I dropped everyone off at Suriya's and the girls divided the fish. One of the girls handed me a bucket. I handed it back to her. Because she was deaf, she spoke with her fingers and I did not understand. One of the other girls repeated what she was saying, translating from sign language.

"Would you like us to clean them for you?" she asked. "No, I don't want it, it's ok," I replied. Suriya told them to keep all of them. I took the trike to Mr. Yee and told him that Suriya would bring him a bucket of fish. As I got to my building, there were two men at the door. One was sitting on a motorcycle with his hands on the handlebars, and the other stood blocking my way. He tilted his head to the left and looked at me. "Take a walk with us," he commanded. The man on the motorbike left. The remaining man pulled his shirt up so that I could see his gun.

"Walk toward the fire-circle," he said. We passed by many people I knew, some smiled and nodded their heads. I wished desperately that I could tell them what was happening to me, but I felt paralyzed. There were many things running through my head: I hoped I would not suffer if they shot me and I hoped Nang Ya would know the cause of my death. Or that someone would see the gunmen and stop them before they shot me. There was no one down at the circle. Down below was the flat field that the children had made into their soccer field. There was a group of boys down there, all between ten and fifteen years old. The man with the gun had taken off his sunglasses and ordered me to walk behind a small bush. There, I saw a dead tree which had fallen, which was crawling with red ants. As I stood beside the tree, the man said: "Put your fucking foot on it, you corpse!" I did as he commanded and he pulled the pistol off his belt, aimed at my right foot. Just as I was about to take my foot off the tree, one of the man put my arms behind my back and handcuffed me. He whispered in my ear: "Don't you ever go to the town again and fuck Nang Ya or you will become a corpse, do you hear me?!" As he let go of me, the other man shot my foot. They pushed me to the ground, took off the handcuffs and left. The bullet had gone right through my foot and into the ground. As I bled, the blood mixed with the dirt and made red clay. I didn't realize how much I was bleeding until later.

The pain hit me a few minutes later. I dragged myself to the field and called to the kids for help. The whole group stopped playing and rushed towards me. Then they stopped and all of them ran away. I had lost so much blood that I felt very dizzy now. A few minutes after they had left me, I saw them returning, running with a group of men and women, a big group, I don't know how many of them there were. One of the women screamed, and then mumbled, "Who on earth could do this to such a young and innocent poor soul?" She took hold of my arm and one man told her to let go. "One thing at a time, sister," he said.

"You don't know what you're doing!" he shouted. Everybody seemed to want to take part in helping me. One man carried me on his back, another took off his shirt and wrapped it around my foot to try and stop the bleeding. As we reached the clinic at the front of the camp, the glare of the sun looked like fire to me; everyone around me was sweaty and dripping. They put me on a long table and a moment later a nurse came in, pushing through the crowd and telling them to go outside. Everyone had moved out, but they stood outside trying to spy on me.

"Were you trying to be a hero, huh? By daring someone to shoot you?" said the nurse? After she had completed her examination, she poured alcohol in the wound, and I cried out. "You are not going to die from this," she said, smiling, as if this were a joke. "Be serious," I said, "it is painful!"

"I am, what do you want me to say, soldier?"

"Don't worry," she said, "we'll fix this for you. You don't need the doctor for this, see, it's just a hole through the bottom of your foot, there's no bullet inside. It's not bad; I thought we would have to cut your foot off." This nurse obviously spoke her mind. After wrapping my foot, she puts her arm behind my back and lifted me up to a sitting position. As she did so, her long, shiny hair covered my face, but she made no apology.

"You owe me twenty baht," she said jokingly. "You are free to go, come back in one week." I left, and the crowd outside was waiting to see how I was doing. One of the men lifted my arm and lowered his shoulder under it and helped me to my room. A few minutes after I entered my room, two teen-aged girls were knocking on the door. Before I could get to the door, they entered, one of them saying: "Miss Valee sent us to give you some aspirin." They looked at one another and smiled, and the second girl said, "Oh, and she sent you this." I took the plastic bag from her, asking what it was. They smiled but did not speak. When I opened the bag, I saw two oranges inside, along with a note. As I took them out, the girls left, and saw them through the gap of the door, running. I limped back across the floor and lowered myself back on the bed and read the note.

"Hi! I forgot to give you aspirin, in case you have pain, don't worry about the cost, the two girls are my brother's daughters. Next time I would appreciate it if you could tell me your name. Valee." Long ago, when I was about eight or nine years old, my aunt used to tell me about first sight. During harvest season, the villagers would exchange their labor in the fields for some of the rice they harvested. One day, while doing this, she went to a distant village, and while she was working in the field, many men and women came to speak to her, but none of them had interested her enough for her to think about them for long after. One late afternoon, a man came walking into the field to which she had been assigned. Throughout the rest of the day, they did not have any contact or speak to one another, but after that day, she thought about him constantly and never forgot him. She said that she felt a great compassion for him, but said that after that day she never saw him again. Her friends made jokes about it, saying that it was love at first sight. She protested, explaining that there were no feelings of love or wanting to marry him, only a feeling of connection. She told me, for unknown reasons that everywhere you go; you will meet people like this, "at least one in your lifetime."

Valee, I thought. It was a pretty name. Interesting and good-looking woman. She was probably three or four years older than I was. Somehow she had triggered the memory of my aunt. Miss Valee's note had given some ease to my mind after all the thoughts of Nang Ya's affair with another man. Valee would never be one to take back her jokes, if you didn't understand them, you might be hurt. I thought back to the group of boys who had gone for help. At first I had been disappointed in them, when I thought they were running away. Without realizing what was in their minds I was frightened about the unknown. The boys might have been eye-witnesses to these criminals doing harmful things, and if the boys had intervened, they might have been followed or killed for having done so; they didn't take the risk, but their compassion remained. Now, however, I realized that the boys hadn't had any capacity to help me in my dangerous situation, and for that reason they had gone to tell the adults. As

I was contemplating all this, I lay on the floor, laughing inside to myself. Lost in thought, the note still in my hand, I fell silent and drifted off to sleep.

Waking up in the morning was quite an effort. I had difficulty walking, the pain was travelling up my legs and there was a great deal of stiffness. Suriya came to the door and didn't say much, but looked worried. He seemed to have known the price I would pay for this situation. "I will speak to Mr. Young," he said. Mr. Young was the camp director. He was educated in France, and has escaped being sent to the concentration camps for intellectuals by taking this position temporarily. Suriya stayed and chatted for a while before class. I felt that he was truly a kind and good friend. My manly ego was gone; I would take any comfort I could get from anybody who showed me kindness and compassion.

"I will see you at noon," he said as he left. Simsung and Vone came by soon after he left, bringing barbecue chicken and rice. They had passed the interview and were due to leave within the next three weeks. They stayed with me for the rest of the morning. After they left, I went to the bathroom and when I returned, there was a boy of about ten years old standing beside the entrance. He handed me a note and left. When I opened the note, I saw that it began: "I have been crying…," so I took it into my room to read it.

"I have been crying for the last few days, I know what happened to you. There are no words for me to apologies, Bo, but I will ask you one favor. Please take care of yourself once you feel better. Do not drive the tricycle; do not be seen in public. Tell only Suriya where you are. Do not come to see me at the school. I will let you know when it is safe for me to come back. If Suriya insists on paying for things you do together, please accept it; there is no reason for you to let your ego guide you there. You are always with me in my mind. NY. I put the note in my notebook and put the book in my bag. I went for a walk all the way across the camp, taking the main dirt road to the football field. I found that someone had dug the bullet out of the ground. I went back to the room, still limping hopelessly, despite the fact that the bullet had passed straight through my foot.

At lunch, Suriya came, he asked if I had had lunch. "No," I said, "I didn't feel like eating."

"Come on," he said, "I'll take you to the stand." We went to eat, and he gave two baht to get me a wooden cane. The man gave the money back to Suriya without a word. Before we had finished eating, the stand owner brought over a real cane from a hospital.

"Do not lose it," he said, "When you don't need it anymore, bring it back to me." As we headed back to my place, Suriya said: "From now on, you will line up for food with the couple from building number sixty, ok? I spoke to Mr. Young and you and Nang Ya are still on the same list, even though you are living apart from one another, for some stupid reason. Don't ask me why, you know it. However, when it is your turn for the interview with the people from immigration from whatever country it turns out to be, you will be called. Wherever you end up living, Mr. Young will know. This is special treatment from the camp, Bo, you are not an average refugee, you are known to the international media because of your work in Laos. Remember, they will help you to escape, and once you are out of here, they will come back to find out about you, the camp will be rewarded for your safe escape. But for now, you are like anyone else, we are like stray dogs. As Suriya left me to go back to class, I burst into tears.

Chapter 10

It was a frightening moment when Mr. Young told me that I must go on hiding. I felt as though I were a murderer who had taken someone's life and was hiding from the eye of the law. In fact it was the opposite: someone else had broken the law in order to fulfill his sexual desire; he had been unfaithful to his lawful wife, and finding that I was a key witness to this fast which could destroy his marriage and his reputation. At first he had warned me by sending his bodyguards to shoot me in the foot, but it seemed clear that he would eventually silence me by killing me. Mr. Young, however, had guessed the governor's plan, and repeated Nang Ya's instructions that I should disappear from the public scene. He looked at me with sympathy, his black moustache hanging long and thin down to his throat, showing his skin underneath; he was a pleasant-looking person, for some reason I saw a picture of Ho-chimin in him. They were both tall and thin, and spoke in proper language; using simple and pleasant words.

"You are like a dog without an owner, son," he said gently, "Nobody can take care of you but yourself."

"I didn't do anything wrong," I protested. "I know," he said. "When you do wrong it is easy to fix, but when someone intends to do you harm, the wrong-doings are many and it is very difficult to fix."

He changed the subject then, starting to explain the plan he had prepared. I was to move from my assigned room to go and live with a couple in the building in the centre of the camp. I would have to be constantly looking for police or civil servants, and try not to let them see me. This would mean not going out during the day. He told me of a couple of places I could go and work in exchange for the day's meals. One of them was at the back of the building which held the boxing ring, locking up the house. But that was only for working, not to live. Another option was to live with his former workers.

The sun was getting higher. It was hot outside as I walked back to my room wearing sunglasses to shade my eyes. Those refugees who could afford to buy umbrellas were walking on the naked street, not avoiding the sun, but simply blocking it by changing the position of their umbrellas, moving them from above their heads down to in front of their foreheads. Each time I passed one of them, I could feel the hot air being pushed away from my body for a moment, only to have it return a few seconds later. By the time I reached my room I was dripping with sweat as usual.

I had left the door open. As I packed up my belongings, my mind wandered from its ordinary functions. The governor should not have complicated the lives of poor souls like Nang Ya and me. He has money and power; he would have been better off taking a young, beautiful mistress from women of his own kind and leaving Nang Ya alone. My mind turned over these thoughts as I finished gathering my things with no stability in my mind.

All of a sudden, Valee came to see me. It was a great surprise. I wondered if she knew of my problems or if she had just happened to come for a short visit. She stood at the door, holding the bamboo door-frame with one hand, as I raised myself up from my knees onto my healing feet. "I didn't expect a visitor, but thank you for stopping," I said. She walked in and put a plastic bag on the bench. "I brought you pineapple cookies. I wasn't sure if you would like them," she said. I invited her to sit on the bamboo floor, which had once served as the sleeping place for Nang Ya and me.

"Did you put paper on the walls?" she asked. "No, my girlfriend did," I answered. "Oh." She ran her fingers over her hair and looked me directly in the eyes. I could tell that she was concerned about whatever little information she had about my situation. I wasn't sure if she knew only a little, or the whole story of my relationship with Nang Ya and her affair with the governor, the whole course of events which had led my life into danger. I didn't feel that I knew Valee well enough to tell her about all these obstacles, but it was possible that from the rumors she had heard, she felt closed to me due to the many defects in my story. I was still much attached to Nang Ya physically and mentally, but there was a slow progression toward my being lured into a new relationship with Valee.

We began to chat about the day-to-day things which two people who were newly acquainted would discuss, but soon were talking about my future life underground. Valee explained that she would work with Mr. Boune Young to maintain my name in the refugee register so that when Nang Ya ended her affair with the governor, I would still be on the list and could then go abroad. It was up to me to consider whether to include Nang Ya's name alongside mine, so that we would be considered as a couple. Otherwise, the camp authorities could determine a separation for me if I should wish, and I could claim a new status as a single man. The new status would be even faster to process, as it would be much easier for the immigration officers to find sponsorship for a single man than for a couple, who were given family status, from a Western country. However, from a humanitarian point of view, if one were sponsored by a church, they would prefer to take a family with children rather than a single person, so my chances remained slim.

When I offered to get us an Oval tine, Valee insisted that she would go and get them. "I need to speak to the stand owner," she said. When she returned, we ate the cookies she had brought. They were delicious and I ate most of them. Before we went to the new room, which I would be living in for the next two years, she gave me a list of people, including her, I could trust and could contact whenever I needed to.

As I mentioned before, there was nothing permanent in the camp: every building, restaurant, boxing ring and cock-fight arena was built of bamboo, and was expected to last no more than one to five years. Anything could be cancelled at any moment by us or by the Thai authorities, and if it wasn't the buildings would rot away. Given this temporary existence I felt like I was one of a herd of water-buffalos in a grassy field: all I did was eat, sleep, have sex and look out for predators. The difference was that the buffalos did not fear their predators until they saw them approaching.

I left most of my unnecessary belongings in the room. All I brought was my English dictionary, my sleeping things and my clothes. Valee carried my bag and I carried the straw floor-mat to my new room. As we walked, Valee asked me if I felt angry about the matter and blamed Nang Ya. The question was odd and I felt uncomfortable, it seemed to me that Valee was acting as a psychiatrist, but too personal, I would never ask anyone a question like that unless I were a professional therapist. Apart from that striking question, Valee was a pleasant woman, in addition to her good looks. She tied her hair in a knot behind her head in the old-fashioned tradition of a house-wife, her skin was light and she had a great sense of humor. She dressed in traditional Laotian clothing: long sarongs and short-sleeved purple silk shirts. On days when she was not working, she wore jeans or other long pants. At other times she looked like a Western teenager, wearing uniforms that conformed to that culture, though we had not yet adapted to it, nor were we even living in it. Having had her with me for a few hours during my time of distress had been a good feeling.

When we arrived at the new place, I ran out of things to say. I was lost in thought and in the fear of being seen by the governor's people who would want to harm me. "I'll see you tonight," Valee said. I thanked her for the company, and before she left, she looked me in the eye and said: "You are a good man, Bo you will always be with me." A second later she was gone, disappearing among the bamboo huts. I thought that her words were unrealistic; it was too soon for her to say such things, things that Nang Ya had said. The words gave my mind no real comfort.

Before I entered the room, I stood near the door watching the children play marbles on the dusty ground. The sounds of a middle-aged man came through the side-walls of the building, and suddenly he shouted: "Come around to the back!" The front door was left open, I had thought to enter there, but followed the man's voice around to the back, where the afternoon sun shone through, everything seemed boiled by its heat. The man was about fifty. He couldn't hold his tongue for a second to allow me to say anything or to explain myself, and did not pause to tell me it is him that I suppose to live with and I met him and his wife before. Once in a while, he would ask: "Do you understand what I am saying?" and all I could do was to answer "Yes," or nod my head. He started by telling me about how his fifteen-year-old son had died of malaria six months earlier, and that the room I would be staying in had been his son's. He and his wife had stayed in their own room and the room was now never used. When his wife appeared, the man fell silent. Before she appeared, I felt as though I was a simple man without morality speaking to a harsh but kind-hearted man I met and knew them both before but did not know the detail of their lives story.

She was my customer from taxiing, Vana. I knew her well, but had not known her husband's name, which was Searth. I had also not known of the loss and their grief over their son until this moment. She and her husband helped me to bring my things into the room. It was dark, and about four feet by six feet. Because I wasn't a large person, the size would not be a problem for me. The door would be at my feet, and therefore if I had to escape I could push the wall either at my head or on either side of me, as they were only made of pieces split bamboo stacked one upon the other. A moment later, Vana returned with ice-water in red and blue plastic cups, and handed me the blue cup. The coldness of the water stopped the sweat from dripping from my forehead.

Mr. Boune Young is a good man," Vana started, and went on to explain how they were close to him and his family. Back in Laos in the late fifties to the mid-seventies Vana and Searth worked for Mr. Young as his private gardeners. Boune Young had a lot of money in a Swiss bank, and didn't have to stay in the camp, but chose to do so anyway in order to help the people who had escaped from Laos to Thailand to be recognised by the UN so that they would be provided with new homes and safety. Boune Young and another high-profile officer from Laos, Dr. Quag, met with former governor Kamphol Klinsukhol of Nongkhai at his home in 1975, after the communists took over Laos. In the meeting, Dr. Quag asked the governor for help in providing temporary land for the refugees. Dr. Quag then left for Paris to continue his campaign to help refugees from Laos, while Mr. Boune Young directed the Nongkhai refugee camp. His goal was to help all refugees to find a new home in the Western world by putting pressure on the UN to find sponsorship as quickly as possible. He felt that the United States was responsible for the refugees. Never in their history had the people of Laos abandoned their land and country until the end of the Vietnam War, due to the United States' involvement.

After that, Vana kept silent. I had felt that having connections with high-profile people was not the way to make your way, it wasn't in my nature to lean on higher people in society; in fact I hated nepotism. However, given my circumstances, I felt at ease. Furthermore, there was still a chance that my name was on the waiting list and remained a priority for interview.

It was a long afternoon. Before she left, Valee had promised to come and see me at my new place that evening. While she was speaking to me, I hadn't paid much attention to whether she would come or not, but once I had finished talking to Vana and Searth, my thought were hardly ever removed from Valee. The words which remained most in my memory were "You are a good man, Bo you will always be with me." I didn't suppose she had meant much by those words, but I turned them over and over in mind while I was alone. Her smile had a great effect on my compassion for her, as did her deep attention to my problem and the vulnerable time I was living through. Internally, I asked myself what she could want from me. I had a girlfriend to whom I felt a great attachment, she had failed me in her need for another man, but had never cancelled the connection of our souls. The calamity between us had brought knowledge of our evolution: half instinctual and half by cultivation. The governor, who was supposed to set an example of good conduct for his people had failed himself with his own weakness in controlling his sexual desire for those who were young and came from a different country, like Nang Ya. She was trapped, and had no power to free herself.

After the sun had gone to sleep, Vana invited me for supper. I was hungry, but didn't feel like taking the time to eat, so I excused myself and went to sit outside in the dark. Searth came out and offered me a cigarette. I declined, but he sat beside me talking about when he was younger, but he saw that I wasn't paying attention and went back inside to Vana. Afterward, my own weaknesses in communication struck me, I needn't have ignored him.

The darkness brought with it colder air. I sat comfortably on the bamboo bench in front of the building and looked at the sparkling lights on the roofs. Around them were all kinds of insects buzzing around, and dead ones stuck inside, looking like black mold. When I moved my eyes away from the lights, I saw that the evening had become darker; I could hardly see a thing on the ground or between the buildings. Then, I saw a flashlight coming toward me, and stood up. "I told you I would be back," Valee said, "How have you been?"

"I couldn't wait to see you back," I told her. She said she had told Mr. Boune Young everything was settled about me and he told her to keep in touch, and not to worry too much. I was told not to appear in public between ten in the morning and two in the afternoon. After sunset, I would be free to go anywhere in the camp; if there was a police patrol, I would be informed for my security. It was around seven-thirty, I asked Valee if she would like to go to the stand, she nods with smile.

We drank beer. The bartender came up behind Valee and said: "Keep him out of trouble, huh, would you?" We all smiled and he told us there was a party at the fire-circle. I could see the whites of Valee's eyes. The stand's owner seemed to have connections with everyone, which helped him to sell more, I supposed. Sometimes it seemed like he was an employee of an information centre or a tourism official, or something of the sort.

"Would you like to go?" I asked, and she replied, "Sure." There were not many young people at the stand; most of the men were over thirty. They were watching boxing on TV, live from Odon. Whenever one boxer hit the other, there were loud and aggressive yells; I saw one of the men stand up, and he stepped on another man's foot. The other man stood up and kicked him in the back, and he fell to the floor, bleeding. The crowd took hold of both men and the bartender turned off the TV for a while. I took hold of Valee's arm and we backed out as I handed the bartender some money. I could feel Valee's hand shaking, so I pulled it around my back and she kept it like that the whole time we were walking to the fire-circle. What had begun as joking between the two men had quickly turned violent. I wasn't sure what had gone through each man's mind, but I was sure that simple men tend to have weak morals. (There were many things in the camp that Thai people were making their money from.)

The place had now changed a bit; it had been a while since I had been there. They had built benches around the fire-pit where before there had only been stones surrounding a small fire. Now there was a larger pit which could hold kilos of wood that would burn for a long time. Behind it was a large and long table where the musicians put their stereo equipment. The group of entertainers called themselves musicians, but I had never seen them sing a single song. Instead, they would put a tape on the large Toshiba radio with tape-player and off they went, with the music turned up to the maximum volume. There were no people living nearby to complain about the noise, but in any case the people at the fire-circle were young, naïve and full of heart. A sad song, "This Rose" was playing. I held Valee's body next to mine: "Shall we dance?" I asked. Without a word, she stood up and we danced. As the song ended, I heard someone shouting "again" repeatedly, and the crowd began clapping; whether it was for the song or for the man who replayed the tape, I couldn't be sure.

As we were holding each other, Valee leaning her cheek against mine, I slowly moved my face to face hers and kissed her deeply. When The Rose ended for the last time, they played a tape of The Bee Gees "Staying' Alive," and Valee did not want to dance anymore. We sat on a bench in a corner which had a large stone behind it which we could lean our backs against and relax. The music was playing full-blast again and people were excited. The benches were all empty now, apart from the one we took. We ignored the crowd and the music and turned our attention to one another instead: we did not speak, but our bodies acted as though they craved sensuality. As I continued to touch her, she pushed my body away and demanded that we leave. I asked her to hold on for another thirty minutes. I looked at the fire and watched it crackling, sending small lights shooting up like fireworks at a New Year's celebration.

As we walked back, our intention was to return to Valee's room, but halfway there we changed our minds. We changed direction and began heading toward the school where Nang Ya and Suriya taught. Inside, there were no lights anywhere, and it was quiet. The only sound we could hear was our own breathing. I took hold of Valee's hands and took her inside. She turned her front toward me and leaned her back against the bench, her breathing sounded as though she had been playing a chasing game. She rolled up her skirt and took off her underwear. I could feel her body shaking without stopping for a second, and at the end she cried out and held me still as though she didn't want to let me go. When I turned to the door, she stood behind me, leaning her cheek against my shoulder and holding me with both her arms. I turned to my right and held her hand as we walked toward the narrow naked street, but in a moment we were standing facing one another and kissing again.

The crickets still chirped, the darkness was the same, but the two of us had become one. There were no words to describe our feelings, there were promises and plans for our future together; we were facing the possibility that we had just conceived a whole new life. We had not paid attention to this possibility, and neither of us had the desire to have a son or daughter, it was simply started by our sexual desire, and our ultimate goal was making love, not only to relieve the unpremeditated sexual desires, but also to receive the joy of our natural sexual body-heat. To regain our energy, we sat on the bench. Both of us were silent, but we held hands and she leant her head against my shoulder, with our thoughts being lost into the mists of the open air. "I wish you could forget Nang Ya," she said.

CHAPTER 11

I went to pick up one of my regular customers in the afternoon for the last time. I explained to her that I was no longer able to drive the tricycle during the day. She seemed to understand, and had heard about my situation, that I had to avoid police and civil servants, but she looked disappointed. She gave me a hundred baht, not for the work I had done, but rather to help me out in my difficult time. At first, I told her that I couldn't accept charity, but she insisted that it wasn't charity money, she was giving me a last-day bonus according to the Buddhist belief that it would cleanse her mind and that she would then live in eternal happiness, but the fact that she was giving the money to me, a living person, was more a sign of her good heart. I shared with her my reaction and reflection, since normally people hang the money from trees to receive that happiness on special occasions. I accepted the money at last, but ignored the reason she had given me. She had convinced me enough, that my pride had left me at the same time as Nang Ya had. My personal life and feelings had become a topic of conversation for those who knew me.

Before I left, she asked if Nang Ya had seen me yesterday. She said that Nang Ya had come into the camp and was looking for me. I said no, and that I had no interest to see her. Later, I thought that I shouldn't have said that. I knew that I was still thinking about Nang Ya and that my customer could see my emotion. She touched my cheek and looked as though she was going to cry.

"Things happen without warning, keep your hope, son," she said. As I turned my wheel to the street, she stood and watched me. I saw her in my rear-view mirror. I had the feeling that I had disappointed many people, and she was one of those. When I arrived at Mr. Yee's, he didn't seem to notice that I was there, he was talking to a man who was complaining about the tricycle, as its chain had fallen off in the street. Because this had caused him to lose money, he didn't want to pay Mr. Yee for that day. I overheard the exchange because he was shouting, as well as cursing and spitting. I could see that I would have to wait, so I stepped out of the shop and stood with my back against a bamboo pole. Syline, Mr. Yee's second daughter, brought me a cup of cold water.

"Thank you," I said, and she smiled. I thought she would go back inside then, but I was wrong. She stood in front of me, holding the rest of the water in a red plastic bottle. "Your friend told me last week that you speak English?" she said. "Yes, a little," I replied. "Would you be interested in teaching me?" she asked. "Maybe, which friend of mine told you that I speak English?"

"Suriya." I had the feeling that Suriya might have a crush on this girl.

Syline was nineteen years old, with light skin, long hair and brown eyes, and was quite shy. In Laos she went to the Leotos Chinese private school which most Chinese children go to, and had studied business at university in Hong Kong. She had then returned to work in the family's own store. The Chinese were known as money vacuums. Syline said that her uncle and cousins were living in Des Moines, Iowa in the United States, so her family had more chance of being sent there to rejoin the family. She wanted to learn Basic English so that when she went to the States, she wouldn't need to wait too long to continue her university studies.

The United States immigration policy for refugees from Asia had three criteria for acceptance: the family, the former employment and the question of whether that person had anti-American feelings due to the Vietnam War. Talking about her university studies, Syline appeared excited. I was paying great attention to her and listening to what she was saying when the old man spoke to me. "Why did you bring it back so early today?" he asked. I handed my cup back to Syline, and she took it and went inside. As she went, I said: "I'll talk to you later."

"I won't be taking it anymore," I told Mr. Yee, and paid him for that day. He didn't ask the reason, but simply scratched his head and spat constantly, in his usual manner. I reflected that a good man does not always have very good manners.

On the walk back, I thought about Syline. She was four years younger than I was and had a great ambition to continue her education. This was in contrast to most young people in the camp, who had lost their interest in education, such as the girl who I had talked to at the fire-circle, who had summed up her life as follows: "Live your life for the moment, eat, sleep, fuck and do drugs." The lack of concentration is not natural, but rather comes about due to the interception of negative external forces. We were all living in the same place, in the refugee camp, but syline was still supported by her parents.

To witness these two types of life, many types, I should say, was driving me to a mesh of human living without a pattern, no culture or system of religion to guide us onto a discernable path. If we all had Syline's initiative and feeling, we could live free, away from the internal negative outlook, and with more desire to be productive. As I approached my sleeping quarters, I broke out sobbing again. I sat on the edge of the floor and felt as though I could no longer process my thoughts to plan what to do next. Becoming lost in thought was a common daily occurrence for me now, and I felt like that feeling would go on forever.

After a year of living in the camp, it was difficult to go on. I had lost two friends; Nang Ya had left me for the governor and said she doesn't love him. She still loved me but had become his sex-slave for money. Weird. Suriya was preparing to leave the camp for San Diego in the United States. I wasn't living in the camp, not like everybody else, who were waiting to leave for a better life, but having been caught by a politician who feared that his criminal act would destroy his family's reputation had silenced me on that matter. The beginning of my problems had no beginning; I was simply a man living with a conscience riddled with infidelity.

Chapter 12

It was calamity in my mind that evening: my heart-rate rose above thirty and I was dripping with sweat. I took off my shirt, staying outside for most of the evening. I hoped for rain, or at least wind, but they never came. Vana came out of the back building wearing a tank-top and a brown sarong. Searth, her husband, was gone to see the cock-fight, and she offered me something to drink.

"Water please," I said. She went back into the building and returned with a container of ice-water. She placed it beside where we were sitting, on a stump, and told me to help myself.

"Listen, Bo," she said. She explained that she and her husband would like to take me to see the monk, but the temple was located about twelve miles from the camp, beyond the limits of the area we were allowed to visit. I told her that I appreciated her concern, but that I didn't want to go. She knew also that it would be a very risky act to try and take me outside of the camp. However, she thought that she had a way of avoiding the public scene and keeping me out of danger from the governors men, who would likely take me away and throw me in the Mekong River, where I would surely drown, making my death look like an accident. This had happened to many people from the camp in the past. The victims were those who had done things which went against the governor's opinions. For instance, a month ago, two boys who had been brought to the governor to work, paint his house's fans in return for food and lodging for a month.

After the job was done, the boys went to the governor and asked to be paid. The governor refused. One of the boys explained to him that the camp director had said that apart from the month's food and lodging, the boys would receive two hundred baht. The governor asked them to stay for supper with him, and at nightfall he ordered his bodyguard to drive them to the south shore of the Mekong, strip them and throw them into the river. The guards did this, and kept their guns pointed at the boys to make sure they swam back to Laos. Because the river was so large, swimmers need something to hang on to when they get tired, like an inner tube or other floating object. Without such a supporting object, no one would survive. The two boys died. A week later, a local found the bodies and called the police. The local paper reported that the victims were two boys who had escaped from Laos and had drowned trying to get to Thailand. The last sentence of the article confirmed that they might have been shot in the head by Lao communist soldiers and killed before they started swimming.

In the camp, a mailman who had permission to travel between the camp and Nong Khai witnessed the crime. A month later he disappeared. Vanna also knew of these stories of things which had happened since the camp was established. When I mentioned the incidents, Vanna moved her body against mine and spoke with emotion, clearing her throat from time to time. She told me, "Whatever you see or hear, of someone disappearing or losing their life, keep it to you." She kissed my cheek.

"It is ok," I said. After we had shared the tragedy which had happened not so long ago in the camp, she held me for a while. Our bodies were sticky, but she didn't seem to pay much attention to that fact, as she was crying, troubled about her son. "He is nearly sixteen by now," she said, rocking me. The smell of her sweat and the odor of her armpits were so great that I had to say something to her. “I’m having difficulty breathing,” I told her. She let go of my body, still crying. I stood up and took off my shirt, wiping off the sweat. She went back to her room. “Let us know if you need anything,” she called as she went.

Chapter 13

The darkness didn't seem to reduce the heat of the hot day. It was in fact less hot, but my body didn't seem to know the difference. Probably the only difference was at the weather office, with their exact measurements. The heat was only a small portion of the factors which were complicating my time, physically and mentally. I was caught in the heat of distress, hiding, I just moved from one building to another like it was no big deal that the governor's people wanted to kill me to silence his problem. This was ridiculous, stupid turning of my mind. However, would any other alternative I had really help me? I felt a pain in my chest and my breathing increased as I stood there alone in the midst of the temporary buildings with narrow spaces between. My mind became a blank and I went to sleep. Instead of crickets disturbing my sleep, their noise was a comfort, without them I couldn't sleep. As my anxieties and worries increased, their humming relaxed me a bit. In fact, my mind was turned to the crickets themselves, living on the ground, with perhaps no food at all.

It wasn't hard waking up in the morning, but I was very tired. A few minutes after the sun was rising, I had an Oval tine. On her way back from jogging, Valee stopped by to tell me that she could only come to see me after work, and she also told me to be ready for Suriya's farewell party that evening. Valee wore a yellow tank-top and long white cotton pants with a rope tied tight below her flat belly. I found it very sexy and as I kept my eyes on her belly, she stared at me. "What now?" she asked, jokingly. "Come inside, I want to talk to you," I said. She put her palm on my forehead, pushing me back, and looked at her watch. "I have to run," she said, and ran off. I watched her from the back as she was running, and missed her. An hour later I couldn't keep my eyes open anymore, so I went back to sleep until noon. Before I fell into a deep sleep, my mind turned over the thought of Valee's body, repeated many times. Her straight, long legs, curved body and butt—I found them sexy, and they drew all my attention in a very striking way. She was a good friend. Now I was facing another dilemma: the sense that there were two women of whom I was fond. I felt as though I had a sin inside me and did not know what to decide.

"Are you there, Bo?" Vanna called from the door. "Yeah, what is it?"

"Seath brought a cattle-tail barbecue, do you want to eat some?" she asked. "Not now," I said, still yearning. "Come and get it when you're ready, I'll leave it on the fire-rake, ok?"

"Ok, thanks," I said.

I took a shower and then went to Vanna's room. She brought rice and chili sauce with the tail, and I ate my lunch there. Outside, most of the buildings smelt of stale urine, and the ground was covered in papers and scraps of left-over bamboo, remnants of people's building and eating. Those dirty surroundings had been a part of my daily scenery, and did not disturb my thoughts while I ate. I was thinking of Vanna and Seath's appearance. Vanna was wearing her favourite attire, a tank top, which left her unshaven armpits exposed, especially when she lifted her arms to reach something above her head. The long, black hair there and her sweaty body caused a great sexual urge in one's imagination. Seath however had more of an appearance of someone who was homeless and suffering from a mental disability. He hadn't shown any ambition to save for the future, instead engaging in gambling activities, cock-fighting and poker, as well as soccer, which people bet money on, but was considered a leisure activity. When he spoke, he rarely talked of plans for the future, and showed no interest in pursuing anything other than drinking, smoking and gambling. For Vanna, on the contrary, every element of human desire was in her conscience: from that for a better life to sexual desires.

I had intended not to judge after only having observed a person. Conversely, perhaps due to my internal calamity, every aspect was worthy of consideration and interpretation, to pass the time and to help to ignore one's own unsolved problems. Times like this were not times to think logically, one could only respond to the mind's branching off in all directions. There was no ending or permanent direction to which the mind would conform; instead it goes like a cotton flower caught up in the wind, away, up and down then disappearing with no trace to the spot where it had dropped. The next day the mind might be like a tent, dark and light in day and night.

An hour after my late lunch, I went to the bathroom, for want of something to do. I found an out-of-date newspaper on the door and read it. There was an article on the third page in which it was written: "Friends can be found everywhere," which I tore out and took to my room. Once there, I took my clothes off and laid down on my back to read it in great detail. The author was a woman, whose name I have forgotten. "Friends are everywhere and everything," she wrote, "from listening to the radio, in classrooms, in workplaces, at social activities, but most importantly through reading." I felt worthy for having spent so much time reading, then.

It was obvious to me that in times of distress, the only friends I had were the characters in the book I was reading. One of them was a biography of Prince Petsarane of Laos, the founder of the country and its leader from 1941 to 1945. Because Japan was allied with Germany and Italy during World War II, fighting against Britain, America and France, in Asia, the Japanese army took over most countries as a protection against the allied countries which had taken them over; in the case of Laos, this was France. Its army invaded Laos and entered its capital city, Vientiane, on March 10, 1945. The leader's political ideology of independence in Laos went against the French, and he fled to Thailand for political asylum and would remain there for more than ten years. The story went on to tell about his interest in hunting and the book he had written about hunting and animal instincts. In reading all this, I found it very interesting, and wondered about my own case. The book didn't solve my problems, but in it I found a friend who had avoided being caught by his opponents for eleven years before he returned to Laos and died at the age of 70. As I put my book down, the calamity in my mind continued. I wished that I did not know that the governor was trying to kill me. I imagined what it would have been like if he had just sent a gun or knife man to do away with me. That would have been it—done without much suffering.

I hadn't had much time to contemplate this when Suriya came to tell me that he would be leaving the camp the following morning at 6 o'clock. We went to the stand for the last time. He had cut his hair that morning and was wearing clean jeans and a blue long-sleeved shirt. He looked a bit nervous, and spoke mostly about himself: his past and his relationship with his grandfather, who was a high-school teacher. We sat at the small brown table in the corner where not many customers would be close by. It was not exactly quiet, but we both ignored the other people's talking. For that moment, Suriya seemed to have forgotten my problem, and he did not ask a single question about how I was doing since Nang Ya had left the camp. Instead, he brought up things from his own memory.

"I was about nine or ten when my grandfather took me fishing," he said. He continued to describe what he grandfather had said to him, which he had been turning over and over in his mind for a long time. One of the things was the metaphor of leaves as human life, "the falling leaves never again returning to the trees." When they fall, some will be carried more or less far away from the trunk, but none of them will ever return. "Do you think we are like the leaves your grandfather described?" I asked.

"Not all of us," he replied, "but many of us seem to fall into what my grandfather described, especially now, I don't think anyone wants to return to his birthplace, because of the political unrest. Even when one is in his or her own country, one has to make a living and needs to move away and plant small seeds wherever one lands. We took our drinks and he continued talking about the United States and what he planned to do in the first couple of years after he got there.

Suriya looked at the two customers at the door. It was a man and a woman in their late thirties, who were holding hands and paying great attention to one another. After a second, he continued where he had left off. The United States is a great country that gives opportunities to everyone who arrives there, he said, it is a place for consumerism if one is willing not to get involved with foreign policy, the policy that gives the right to the government to intervene in a small nation and their problems. The Vietnam War was a good example; in the early 60s the United States used the attack in the Gulf of Tonkin as a sign that the Chinese communists would take over, so to protect national interests, the US sent troops over to protect its friend, but in reality the attack in the Gulf of Tonkin and the Russian submarines would come to protecting north Vietnam but latter those things never happened. War to the United States is a reason to create jobs and to make money for large corporations which make weapons and food supplies, which therefore kept more jobs for the country's people. "It is good to not know too much," he said. He sipped another drink. "I will work, maybe one to three years, and save some money, and then I will go back to school to study business administration." We left the stand, and I said "See you tonight."

"Come early, ha!" he exclaimed. He put his head down and walked away. Whether it was true or not, our discussion had come to a sensible conclusion about the United States government, as far as we knew. Perhaps America had gotten involved in wars in smaller nations for other reasons we could not know, our small talk give a great hope, inspiration and knowledge to me and in the sense that I was be able to talk and friends.

Chapter 14

Suriya was holding a red plastic glass of white whiskey. A couple of friends of his were standing around him. The room was too small to sit, and all the invited guests had to stand around outside in the dark. Actually it wasn't completely dark, since the security light wasn't far away from Suriya's sleeping quarters. Every hundred feet or so along the building there was a pole which stood high above the roof and shone the light out onto large areas, since there were no lights installed in the tiny rooms. Suriya politely took Valee's hand and brought her close to him. "After I am gone, I want you two to stick together," he lectured her. "Don't worry, we will," Valee replied. "If we're still alive!" I shouted over to them,

He said that as soon as he arrived in San Diego and had a permanent address he would write to us. He also said that he would try to convince his sponsor to bring us to America as well. I thanked him for his care and told him that he had been a good friend to me since I had arrived in the camp. We were both feeling emotionally broken and fell silent. Valee brought us another drink and the three of us left the group to go behind the building and sit on a bundle of dry bamboo. One of Suriya's friends came over and asked permission to play a cassette, saying that someone had brought a tape-player. Suriya gave him permission, and as our conversation continued, the music got louder. The laughter started and people had gone wild—dancing and singing along with the music, which included "Dancing

Queen," among others. "I will miss you guys a great deal," Suriya said, "but life has to go on and let the past out."

He said he had enjoyed hanging out with me, and that he had a great empathy for my situation, saying that it shouldn't have happened that way. When he started talking about my stress about my past relationship, Valee walked away and joined the rest of the crew. She was dancing alone, most of the men invited had a great respect for Valee, they all knew that she was a volunteer nurse at the camp clinic, and that she also had a good connection with the international aid workers who had great influence in the Thailand branch of the UN for refugee resolution. Her appearance gave warmth and hope too many. One of the girls introduced herself to Valee and they went and chatted in Suriya's tiny room.

Suriya and I walked back to the crew. Valee came out of the room and we danced. After a while, they changed the tape. While it was silent we heard a motorcycle on the main street a few hundred feet from us. Suriya shouted to the crew to stop the music right away and told Valee and me to leave. "For your own safety, Bo, go! And do not come to the bus tomorrow morning," he told me. We said goodbye for the last time. For a moment I felt uneasy as we left, and I broke into tears. Valee led me to my sleeping-room and stayed with me for the rest of the night.

Suriya came and banged on the door at 4 am and said that he couldn't sleep and wanted to see me before he left for the airport. I told him not to come into the room. He was silent. It took Valee and me a few seconds to find our clothes as we felt around on the dirt floor. Valee told me to get out of bed and find our clothes, I told her to get up, but she said that she didn't want me to see her bottom. I said that I wouldn't see it because it was still dark, and at that point Suriya banged on the door again to be sure that I hadn't gone back to sleep without saying a last goodbye to him. Finally Valee got up to find our clothes and that was the first time I saw how beautiful her body was, even though I only saw it in the dim light of the new day. She put on her dress and I put on my clothes, and she went back to sleep as I went to the door. I went out shaking my head and smiling.

"Goodbye, buddy," he said, and I said goodbye to him and we hugged one another. Suriya left Nong Khai refugee camp in Thailand in August 1979 at 6 am, and during the same month, Nang Ya was arrested for murdering a police officer, and my situation worsened.

Chapter 15

I was brought for questioning in the camp at first. The camp director asked me to come into his office in the morning a day after Nang Ya was arrested. I walked in feeling frightened, my mind wasn't thinking straight and my mouth was dry. I felt my blood rushing through all my body's nerves, which seemed to explode out as the director asked me to sit. He too looked pale, and he had sticky saliva on the corners of his lips.

"I'd like you to know, Bo," he said, "Nang Ya was arrested yesterday for murdering a police officer in a hotel room. The details will be confirmed later today, now she is in police custody in Nong Khai. The police investigator is on their way, they asked me to bring you in for questioning. I don't have any skills to help or comfort you, but don't worry too much and getting sick. I can ask the international aid workers and human rights workers for refugees from Bangkok to come to the preliminary hearing. You will be a witness for Nang Ya, ok, and from now on I don't want you to worry about the governor, you will be on the human rights criminal protection list."

Mr. Boun Young then asked me many questions and told me to tell the police what I had told him, and not to change the story. I was questioned many times the day after Nang Ya was arrested. They were simple questions: verifying my identity and relationship with Nang Ya. "When did you first meet Nang Ya?"

"In June, 1978."

"Where?"

"In Bueng gane Police Station."

"Do you remember the date?"

"No."

"What was your relationship with her after you met her?"

"A few days after we met, we kind of liked each other and we began a love relationship."

"Did you have sex with her then?"

"Once."

"After that, what was your and her status coming into the camp?"

"We came into the camp as a couple."

"The record shows that you came into the camp at the end of June, 1978."

"That is correct; I don't remember the date, though."

"It is ok. I don't think it is necessary. I believe the police will ask you more questions about what you knew about her activities in town, out of the camp, be prepared for that. I am not in the position to ask you those questions; my job is to build statements in your profile, mostly for your lawyer to make an argument in court." Someone came to the door holding a notebook in his hands. Mr. Boun Young told me to go with him. "Come see me when you come back this afternoon!" he shouted.

I had no idea where they would take me. Outside the building was a red Toyota pickup waiting, filled with boxes of cooking oil. The man urged me to get on the back, so I sat on a box and was driven to the distribution station. As I stepped down there was a crowd of people surrounding the truck. The man told me to jump back on and hand him the boxes one at a time. He opened the boxes and another man, the driver of the truck, took bottles out of the box and gave them to the people. When the truck was unloaded, the man standing on the ground stuck up his hand for me to shake. "I am Larry Bromence, and this is Puchine," he said.

I shook both of their hands. He told me that I would be working with them. We drove back to the camp office, but they told me to stay in the truck while Mr. Bromence went inside. He returned with a white sheet of paper and gave it to me, and told me to sit in the front seat with them. As we left the camp I had no idea where we were going, but the one thing I had in my mind was, I am safe from being shot by the governor's bodyguard. Mr. Bromence told me to read that paper. It was a confirmation that I was hired to work as an assistant for international refugee aid workers. Bromence explained my duties: I would hand out supplies to refugees and sometimes I would work as a translator, as needed.

In the afternoon, after they drove me back to the camp, I went to the office to see Mr. Boun Young. He asked me if I had eaten, and I told him that I had eaten at the restaurant in town. He explained that I wouldn't be paid to do the job I was doing, but that they would pay my living expenses and would provide for my safety. The last thing he told me was not to lose my identification papers as I left for the clinic. Valee had gone jogging with her co-worker Aphai. I sat on the front steps reading An war sadat's biography which I had brought with me everywhere I go, until suddenly they appeared, running toward me side by side. I stood up.

I felt a bit uncomfortable with Valee spending so much time with Aphai, but I did not mention anything to her. Aphai left and told her he would see her sometime after work tomorrow. I had just come to let her know about my day, and left to go back to my sleeping place when she went to have a shower. We didn't talk much; I was drawn into a mood of not wanting to do anything. instead, I slept, and was n't woke up with the horrified feeling about the circumstances without consequences. I hadn't done anything wrong, and so it didn't seem right that I should be living under the criminal protection. The sun was setting and it was time that I stop trying to rationalise everything.

The next morning, the guards who had been posted to the camp were changed for new ones. The man from Nong Khai district who was responsible for the camp and Mr. Boun Young's friend were no longer to be seen coming in and out of the camp. The rumor began to spread that the governor was under investigation by the police for corruption and involvement in running brothels and prostitution rings. I waited for the pickup without really being aware of my surroundings, and went to work. I loaded supplies from the warehouse in town and unloaded them in the camp. When they came, Larry told me to be prepared for tomorrow, as he had received a letter saying that tomorrow at ten o'clock he would take me to see Nang Ya before I was taken in for questioning. We drove along the high way with both truck windows rolled down, the wind cutting off the sound of our words, so instead of shouting to each other, we were silent. I thought about the good deed of the UN officers who made things happen by allowing me to visit Nang Ya before the police questioning, and I wondered what this was all about. At the same time, I was feeling a bit frightened. I didn't have any desire to see her, but at the same time, I felt a great compassion for her.

The warehouse was located a few blocks from the governor's house. It was a building with two storage areas, a residence on the second floor and long rooms on the first floor facing a narrow street in the front, which was mostly quiet. In the back, it faced on a large paved ground onto which we backed our truck, right up to the wide steel door. Inside it was filled with large bags of rice, boxes and boxes of cooking oil, rolls and rolls of floormats, blankets, boxes, and many other things. The ceiling was about twenty feet high, but the stacks of boxes nearly reached it. After we had loaded the pickup, Larry signed a paper which lay on a long hardwood table where two men were sitting and chatting to one another. There was no fan to cool the room, so the two men were shirtless and sweating, the sweat dripping like water from their foreheads, noses and behind their ears. Seeing them sweaty, I knew I must be soaked with sweat myself and I pulled up my t-shirt to dry it. Larry always wore shorts and a short-sleeved shirt with a white towel around his neck, which he would use from time to time to wipe off the sweat, or he would soak it in cold water.

Before leaving the warehouse, Larry brought us some cold Pepsi-Cola. We sat on the tailgate and drank it. He wandered over to the shade of the mango tree, but I stayed still where I was. I was back in the time when Nang Ya and I first arrived in the camp years ago. The heat was boiling our bodies that day too, but in my mind all that was left were the pleasant moments, I heard her cry again that and ask that I hold her and not let her go too soon. I did not see Larry anymore, just Nang Ya, and I began to move very slowly.

"Let's go!" he shouted at me. Puchine did not talk much except for the occasional few words to do with work. He gave us the opinion that next time we should begin before sunrise to avoid the heat. Larry replied that these were good ideas but that there were many procedures which must be followed, as we would have to convince the Thai authorities to open the camp, and tell the refugees to pick up their supplies earlier and convince all the workers related to the project to do the same. It would be more work. Puchine, instead of challenging this or making conversation, went away in silence. Larry said a few words in Thai. I wondered if Larry would come with me to the prison the next day and when the hearing would take place, but I decided not to mention either of these things, and to carry on going with him where I was told to avoid being killed. Knowing I would have the privilege to visit Nang Ya, the day seemed to stretch longer as sunset approached. I remember saying a few things to Larry, and thinking a lot about Nang Ya and how she was.

Chapter 16

The distance from Nong Khai to the prison was about the same as to the camp, about thirty minutes driving, however we headed north. From the camp, we drove through the town and took the small road which began parallel to the Mekong for about ten kilometers. Then we turned left to go west to Odon. I no longer remember the name of the road or of the prison, but the scenery remains captured in my memory; the beauty of the fields, I recorded it in my mind.

The rice paddies lay alongside the road and beyond as far as the eye could see. Because it was harvest season, we could see only harvested, or grounded, straws remained on the fields, the grains had been removed from the straws, sometimes days or weeks before. I wasn't interested in any of these scenes of nature along the road, I was thinking about the problems in which I was involved, I had no faith whatsoever in the existence of something divine. My instincts had gone beyond any religious thoughts, I felt that religion could be just a system created in someone's mind to hold on to and prolong life. I wondered what Nang Ya would think of her ordeal. Since we hadn't seen each other for almost a year, I had lost my attachment to her; however my compassion for her had become even greater. My mind kept slipping from one angle to another, from compassion to all the details of Nang Ya's chronology.

At first, I saw barbed-wire fences. The entrance was a dirt track off the main road, running for about a half-kilometer through the prison lawn. There was no sports facility, in front there only coconut trees and yellowing grass that looked as though it had never been mowed. Larry told the driver to park our pickup in the parking lot, which stood to the side and was a dusty patch of ground with a couple of cars in it. Beside it were many bicycles, and groups of men stood around them, smoking and chatting. We entered the building and Larry gave the warden a paper, which he glanced at and then handed back.

"Come on this side," he said. The door to the left was grey steel gate with a padlock on it the size of a cigarette package. I went in while warden held the door open. He seemed very relaxed, and spoke in monosyllables without eye contact or any evidence of humanity. "Take all the time they allow you, Bo, we'll wait for you," Larry said.

As I approached the prisoners' area, the warden told me to go into the office at the right. The officer there came out of the room and examined my clothes. He examined my shoes and my belt, and for some reason told me to open my mouth while the warden waited. Then he pointed toward the warden, who opened the gate, which I went through. I had hoped to sit next to Nang Ya so that we could express our emotions with physical contact, but it wasn't as I had thought. There was a wall with glass running across the middle, and on either side of the glass were black bars about the thickness of a man's thumb. I was instructed to sit on a gray metal stool with a brown top and wait. The glass looked to be about two inches thick.

"When you hear a bell ring, stop talking. I will come and take you back outside," the warden said, and left. I sat down on the stool as I was told. When Nang Ya emerged and came toward the glass accompanied by two female guards, I could hardly tell if it was her. She looked larger through the glass, until the guards sat her down across from me. First she leaned her head against the glass to have a closer look at me. It struck me at first that she didn't appear to be sad, stressed or worried about her situation, but that she had a big smile and looked to be excited to see me.

"How did you get here?" she asked, putting her hands through the tennis-ball-sized holes in the glass to reach me. I held them for a while with a great compassion for her. "The aid-workers brought me here."

"Thank them for me, they are such civilized beings," she replied. "What happened?" I asked, "Did you do it?"

"Yes."

"Why?"

"It is a long story, but I think I owe you to tell you, Bo, before I am hanged."

"No one will hang you," I told her, but she broke down crying. That was when I realized that the situation was actually terrifying her. "You know I love you, it was always more important to protect you than it was to protect myself."

"Why was that?"

"Please forgive me…because they had the capacity to kill you. For me it was preferable to lose my reputation as a woman than to lose you. I might never have a husband, but at least we would both be alive. I knew that you knew that. I had told you what happened the day that we met, remember?"

"I don't have anything to forgive you for, you didn't do anything wrong, you just left me, I just never understood why." She fell silent for a moment.

"I will tell you why, but then we might not have time for me to tell you everything from the past. I will also give you my notes each time you come."

"Tell me what you can and when I come back next time you can continue," I encouraged her. We could only reach each other with our fingers. "Do you remember what I told you when we first met two years ago?"

"Yes, but I thought that was over," I answered. "It was over for a little while, but inside me it was not. You know, when your face gets burnt, soon it will heal, but you will never look the same."

"He came to the governor's house for a meeting about recruiting more girls from refugee camps as prostitutes. The whole state is making money from us. I didn't remember him," she said. "Who do you mean him?" I asked, forgetting about what she had told me. "I mean my rapist." I stared and felt angry as I waited patiently and listened.

"He told me to meet him at the motel that night or he would tell the governor who I was and I would be sent to the shore like my friend. He gave me a note with the address of the motel and the room number. After he left that afternoon, when I was alone, what he and his friend did to me came flooding back into my mind like it was yesterday: every word they spoke, every movement they made returned vividly to my mind. I realized that this was the opportunity I had been waiting for. I had an idea that had never occurred to me before, that I wanted to kill him." Her tears dripped down on her cheeks, and I was silent for a while. She was silent of words, the only sound was her sniffing to hold off the dripping of her nose.

She went on telling me what had happened. To save time, she spoke non-stop. She wanted to see him too, after she learned that he was the one who had brought up the idea of gang-rape. She did not even know his name but she told me to read the local newspaper on Sunday so I would find out. She went on. She went to the motel, arriving around 7 pm. She had never thought that the time would arrive. She entered the motel, ignoring the receptionist. She noted that it was common practice when a man was waiting for his lady in a hotel room, she would come in and nobody would notice. She went up to Room 210, still holding the slip of paper with the room number written on it. She turned left when she got to the top of the staircase and knocked twice on the door. He opened it, smiling at her. He wore jeans and a long-sleeved black shirt, open at the chest to impress her. "If I had had a gun, I would have shot him right there, she said, tears still clinging to her eyelids. She stayed calm, however, took a deep breath, and smiled back, thinking about how she would do it.

"I'm glad you came, hope you don't hate me," he said, his eyes on her, filled with lust and the creativity of his sexual fantasies. She smiled. "I've lost my hatred for someone who once fucked me in so many ways I liked, and I've been dreaming of fucking that person again the same way," she said, untruthfully, but still somehow seductively. In that moment, the anger she felt was enlarging the air inside her body, pressing the blood up into her veins, which felt like they could explode at any time. She managed to control her emotions; however, one of her thoughts was of her mother's advice that forgiving and forgetting the past would bring out one's happy soul. She then thought this was not a thing to forgive or forget it is a dead experience; she had died that day when he had raped her. She thought that even a white saint would fly and fight with that devil. He had destroyed her womanhood; she could keep her love promise and make sure he was destroyed. However, to show him her anger would probably alarm his devil mind, and he might kill her before she got her chance to kill him.

She stepped inside. "Thank you for inviting me," she said in a diplomatic tone. His eyeballs twitched under his eyelids. His lust blinded him to the signs of danger and he did not think for a second that she might be pretending. "No problem. I'm sorry about what I did to you back then." She knew the apology was not real, but rather made in the hope of fulfilling his sexual fantasies about her, to calm her so that he could have consensual sex with her and not have to rape her. He thought this would give him more pleasure.

"Come," he said, without realizing that his lady was also his enemy. What a man of ignorance, his innocent mind accidently spoke, but the devil inside him remained, and was about to be burned at last. She knew what she wanted. If he hadn't had a gun which she now planned to turn onto his own soul, she would have used the kitchen knife she had brought with her. She had selected the sharpest one, and made sure that it would be large enough to push through his dark skin without complication. She knew that she wasn't strong enough to use anything but the sharpest knife to cut the head off this devil.

"My human mind and instincts seemed non-existent," she said to me, her tears still dripping, and her nose still running. I too was crying as she told me what happened next that night. She spoke to him. "Actually, I don't remember you that well, but after you made me enjoy it so much, I always remembered it: The way you touched me; you didn't kiss me, but you held both of my legs up, you did it with passion and lust. I loved it and I dreamed about it every day, wanting you to do it again."

"A Japanese staff!" he said. "I am sorry, I didn't really want to do it that way, but my friends insisted, that was the only way to do it as a group. We knew that if we asked your consent, you wouldn't give it, and that you would cause more trouble."

"There was one thing I was disappointed about, though," she said, looking into his eyes. "What?"

"I had a dream that it was only the two of us that night. I wouldn't have gotten hurt, and it would have been more fun." He smiled, confirming that thought. "Now it is just you and I," he replied, "and I will do anything to please you, ok? Forgive me that night."

"What happened to my friend? I would like to see her if possible."

"Maybe later I will bring you to visit her, now she is living in Bangkok," he said. "Thank you," she said, and changed the subject, knowing that they had killed her. "Are you going to order us anything to drink before you make me crazy again?"

He laughed joyfully. "You are well-trained, ha? Certainly, I will be back in a few minutes." He walked out the door. "After he left the room, I took my clothes off, but left my underwear on. I hid my sharp knife under the mattress on the left side, where I was planning to lie, thinking that while he was on top of me I could reach my right hand for it and pull it out and push it through his chest," she said, blowing her nose. "After the preparation, I walked to the door and waited for him. Because it was a cheap motel, there was no phone to order room-service, one had to go down and get them, not even from the motel itself, but from a nearby store. It took him a while to return, giving me time to plan how to end his life.

"I heard his footsteps coming and I opened the door. He was shocked to see me without clothes. "You really want this, ha?" he said with a grin. "Yes," I said, "make sure you do it well, bull." He pushed me toward the bed and put the wine bottle on the table with the lamp. He started to kiss my neck. I could feel his erection on my belly, he was taller than I was. I pushed him back.

"Relax, I want to have a drink first, and I don't want you to go too fast, you will be on the bottom first and then we'll switch," I commanded him. "What a girl!" he exclaimed, "I'll do anything you say."

"Good." He didn't seem to have a clue about whether or not I believed him.

We were sitting on the bed and drinking out of the bottle. He took some first, and then I did, but I did not swallow any of it. In the end, he was the one who drank the whole bottle, but he was so strong and filled with lust and passionate about me that he began pulling off his jeans. I helped him to take them off and that was when I found the gun he had at his waist. I picked it up and looked at it, trying to figure out how it worked. "Oh, this is the real stuff," I said. "Be careful, it is loaded."

"But how can you fire it?" I asked. He took my hand and said, "See this, on the back? If you hold it, it is right on your thumb, and this is the thing you pull up before you pull the trigger." I found him to be so innocent, it reduced my anger. But it was too late now; I had decided to do it. "Can you kill deer with this kind of gun?" I asked, feigning ignorance "You could," he replied, "but this is not the type you would use to shoot deer, there is another type. This is for the police, and sometimes the bad guys have it too."

"Ok, so you are the good guy, ha?" I put the gun down beside him on the right and took off his underwear. "I am a law-abider," he replied. "Close your eyes, I am a shy girl," I told him. He did so, and held my back with both hands. "Shy is the best," he said. In my mind, the shyness was long gone; I was a dead-alive person. "Open your mouth and suck your thumb," I ordered him. He did it, with excitement, and I pushed my thumb into his mouth as well, to open it wider, and while me distracted him with my left hand, my right hand picked up the gun. To make him keep his eyes closed, I pulled down my underwear and took his hand to make him touch it, and then touching his forehead. This is to insult him, I thought. I kept talking to him, telling him to keep his eyes closed. At the moment when his excitement reached its height, his mouth opened wide, so I slipped the barrel of the gun into it and continued my dirty talk.

"What the fuck is this?!" he shouted. I grabbed the bed sheet and covered his face before pulling the trigger. I saw blood soaking the sheet and moved away to avoid getting blood on myself, tossing the gun toward his body as I went. I don't know how many bullets went through his throat; the police would later tell me there were six of them. I put my clothes on and went to the bathroom to wash my face. I walked out of the building, passing the empty reception desk. I hit the street at about 9 pm, it was a Saturday night and many people and tricycles were jamming the street near the movie theatre. I took a taxi to the camp. I slept at Vone's place until Sunday morning and then went to see Mr. Boune Yang to tell him what had happened, to tell him that I had killed a police officer.

It seemed so unreal to me that my rapist had gone along with my dirty talk; he was a police officer, well-trained, he should have known better than to get involved with my dirty courtship. But he didn't, his lust was greater than anything else, and in the end he died from it.

"When I first got to Vone's place, I asked about you. She told me you were with someone else. Please don't get me wrong, I don't ever blame anything on you, she said you always told her that you missed me terribly. I cried all night, I couldn't sleep. Mr. Boune Yang asked me to tell him what had happened and asked if I had killed the officer. I confessed that I had. He contacted UN aid workers, human rights representatives and a lawyer for me, and they all came to the camp before the police did. I am being watched by those people now, or else I might be just another corpse floating in the river.

"I thought Mr. Boun Young would help me, and send me away into hiding, but he didn't," she sobbed. "Then I saw four police cars following an unmarked black Toyota sedan, with a cloud of dust following them. They told me that I was under arrest for killing an innocent police officer whose duty it was to protect people…they went on with words I don't remember. I was shaking and could not control my bladder—I wet myself. They handcuffed me and took me to the Nong Khai police station. I was there for three days before they brought me here.

Before I left, I asked Nang Ya why she had left me. She answered, "I had witnessed communist forces handcuffing my father and dragging him out of the house. He shouted back to me that if I were ever to escape the country, I should never come back. I haven't seen him since. I left you to protect you from being killed. This is serious, Bo, the gang is so huge, Mr. Boune Yang is also living in fear, and I don't know how the international aid workers can protect us. Live your best, if you have to marry someone to get out of the camp and Thailand, do it, don't worry about me, I was dead a long time ago, ever since the day I left you."

I had never cried so much as I did that day. As she walked back to the cell, I watched her, the black uniform she wore made it look as though there could be no life underneath, but my mind was still caught on her words, I was dead the day I left you.

CHAPTER 17

The hot summer months and the dry season went by quickly, and the rainy season started again. The Mekong rose up and filled the shoreline. The plants on the shore became green again. The bull-rushes were taller than the other plants and when the soft wind passed by the bounded along as if they had nothing holding them, just going whichever way the wind blew. They were vulnerable plants; when the dry season returned they would disappear for months. Nature is like that, dying in one season and then returning in the next, repeating as our lives do, though we never return to youth again. I am twenty-five now, and have no physical goals set, only ones in my imagination, like a dragonfly, with no place to call home, landing on one blade of grass and then another, and being killed by a predator, if not dying of its own accord. Nature had once been my inspiration, but now it was merely scenery to my thoughts.

I was questioned by the police several times after visiting Nang Ya in prison, but the questions were mostly about my identity and how serious my relationship with her was. After one session of questioning that took place in the district police station, my lawyer told me not to say anything to the police about what Nang Ya had told me about the motel, though he knew that I wouldn't have said anything anyway. The lawyer said that the police would never have a chance to torture me in order to make me speak, since I was being watched by the international aid workers. The good news was that now the crime had become public.

At first, the police asked me to describe her behaviour during the time we were together. The police seemed to be focusing on the possibility that Nang Ya was taking illegal drugs. I said that I had never seen her take any, or known if she was addicted. I omitted to mention her occasional strange behaviour. I thought perhaps it was only natural that someone with more sexual experience participated more. The interrogator eyed me and said, "We don't want your opinion."

The room in which I was questioned was much like a workplace canteen: a large room with no windows and a low ceiling edged by neon lights. The room smelled terribly of cigarette smoke. I found myself irritated by my interviewer—after each question he asked, he would stare down at his yellow-lined pad of paper, looking at his notes, and blinking rapidly. He seemed to be suffering from a headache or something of that nature.

"You. You...You still love Nang Ya, don't ya?" he asked."

"No, I have a new girlfriend." At that moment I realised that I had only compassion for her. But why would the police want to know my personal feelings? At the next interview, which was scheduled a few days later at 10 am, he continued with the same questions about whether I still loved Nang Ya. I didn`t find the question relevant to the murder case. I said "No, sir." He then asked me to describe everything I knew about her, the most important being whether she had ever told me that she would kill the policeman and why.

I learned later that the interrogation was something of a psychological evaluation of Nang Ya. My description was nothing close to their idea of her mental state; I described her as an ordinary, attractive and intelligent young woman. I admired her life story and her accomplishment of finding a career as a teacher. She was loving, kind and filled with hope of prosperity for her future life. She had always spoken of her dream to teach children, especially the poor. Her own life was full of learning, "learning on the run," as we call it, studying while working to make a living. I realised that many of the questions were made up to surprise or frighten me so that I would talk.

"No, sir, she never talked about killing a policeman or anybody else," I answered him. "I want you to tell us the truth," he said. It struck me that while I had been making an effort to think clearly and to try and recapture my memories of what I had seen, known and understood of Nang Ya, when I had described it to him it must have sounded vague. "I know that she told you she killed the officer. Thank you for your cooperation; we need more detail and the sequence of her behaviour the next time." The interrogator put all his papers in his brown briefcase and walked out the door.

The next day, Mr. Broman brought me to the lawyer's office, which was full of a dark, shiny smoke like the fumes of a charcoal burner. In spite of the heat, he was wearing a fake silk shining eggshell-coloured suit. It had a stiff collar, but no tie, and made him look like the American singer Elvis Presley. After Mr. Broman left the room, going out to the reception area to wait for me, the lawyer explained to me that I wasn't a suspect, only a witness, and that I didn't need a lawyer. However, because Nang Ya's case was being examined under special circumstances, as she was an illegal immigrant but under the supervision of the UN as a refugee, I would be dealt with as a witness and suspect alike. Therefore, I would be involved with the trial until the very end. He concluded by repeating that I shouldn't tell the prosecutor anything about Nang Ya's negative behaviour, and encouraged me to keep the same story as I had told the police investigators before. I nodded, and walked out the door, wondering what he meant when he said "a witness and suspect alike." I wondered how effective or serious the international organisation could be to this cause.

"Ready to work now?" asked Mr. Broman. "Sure," I said, but I felt like I had ice on my head. Once we were approaching the highway, where the traffic lights stopped, we started to talk. "I just have a personal question," Mr. Broman started. "Do you still want to bring Nang Ya back with you once the trial is over?" I was silent, thinking about what I wanted to say and trying to understand my own feelings. I was not sure she would survive the prison. "You don't have to share if you don't want to," he said quickly. "Oh, no, it's not that," I said. "Good." He looked at me and smiled. "Where is the driver?"

"He is driving another truck today he went to Bung gane to pick up another new arrival, we might be working on our own for a couple of weeks."

"Why is that?"

"Because our coordinator in Bangkok assigned me to be with you during the murder investigation and perhaps through to the end of the trial."

"Do you people have to do that for a refugee?"

"In reality, we don't have to, however, part of the UN's mission is to protect human life, to bring justice and also to respect the law of the country we are in, providing that law does not violate human rights regulations. In this case, we made our own decision about what to do," he replied. He went on to explain about other cases in many countries in the world, such as in Africa and Latin America, where the UN had neglected to help and many people had been wrongfully convicted or simply killed instead of standing trial. The legal system in Thailand is based on the civil law system, with influences from common law. However, it is known as one of the countries in which enforcement of the law is dry, and corruption is everywhere, and it is important for international human rights advocates to get involved in the cases of immigrants facing criminal charges.

After a short silence, he rolled down the window for some fresh air, and then patted my arm. "Everything will be ok," he said and then began talking again. "You know, I'm beginning to know you personally. I wasn't quite sure what he meant, but my mind was on the fact that he and so many others who had grown up in less-violent, well-educated industrialised countries had a soul to do charity work, so I said as much. Then I felt as though I had been talking too much, and suddenly felt very uncomfortable with my accent in English, especially when he kept having to say "I beg your pardon?" which led me to see that he wasn't always quite sure of my comments either.

"You're doing fine!" he would say, and then would add politely that he should be learning more Thai or even Lao. I didn't know his daily schedule, most of his time seemed to be broken up by accompanying me to different jobs. We arrived at the camp at lunch and had a quick meal of noodle soup before heading over to the Catholic hall. Mr. Broman introduced me to Mr. Myer, whose congregation called him Brother Jean. He was from France but spoke good Thai. For some reason, the majority of the members of his congregation were young people, aged between sixteen and twenty-five. Later that day I would learn that most of them were former students who had left Laos without completing their studies. During the service, which we also attended, the talk was of the history of religion: of Calvinism, Lutheranism and the Protestant faith. I could not find the relation from these topics to a basic service offering comfort to the members of the congregation in need of moral and spiritual clarification in order to continue waiting to live in productive society again. The preaching was more of an intellectual lecture, but it was interesting. Before we left the hall, Brother Jean recommended that Mr. Broman bring me to the hall more often. As we walked outside, dark clouds emerged, but the dust from the streets continued to rise up, making both of us spit constantly.

"I'll see what I can do," he replied to Brother Jean. We drove back to the camp office and he let me out. "See you tomorrow," he said, and drove away. I went into the office. Mr. Boune Yang wasn't there, so I told the woman at the front desk that I had finished early. At that moment, my only desire was to see Valee.

Chapter 18

Valee was having a busy day in the clinic. The doctors were gone for a meeting in Nong Khai and had left many things for the nurses to do; everything except examinations. Many patients, most of them children, had been brought to the clinic with stomach pains, and some of them had even died there. It had been a difficult day and difficult few weeks, she was feeling a great deal of grief and stress. When she came home, she embraced me and seemed happy that I was home, but after supper, her attitude changed as we spoke about Nang Ya's trial.

"I thought you were done with her," she said, raising her voice. "What are you talking about?"

"Don't bullshit me; I know what you think and how you feel about her. You are not with me, Bo, you are with her; you are here because you need me, not because you love me. You love her!" She started sobbing.

When I first met Valee, I had great respect for her, as she was a level above the average person who didn't have a profession. I realised now that she was another woman, a woman who was feeling a great deal of care and love for me. I didn't know what I had done. Maybe she was right, maybe I still loved Nang Ya.

"I am sorry, you're right, I'm done with her, but I had to go and see her because they want me to talk to her during the processing of the trial."

"I said don't bullshit me, who is this 'they' you keep talking about?"

"The aid workers."

"It was you who asked a favour from them, because they accepted you as one of their employees, that's why they're doing it, bringing you to your ex, or no, I'm sorry, your only loving girlfriend!" she shrieked.

I was silent, unable to find the words to explain, only hoping that she would eventually understand the complications I was facing, and that she would not do something shallow-minded like going and sleeping with her co-worker, the gay-boy Aphai. If that ever happened, I thought that anything between her and I would be over, and that in the future I would never find my way back into productive society, and I felt old already. I took the bag of cookies that I had brought home and left, walking along the dusty street with no destination. I didn't feel like going back to my own sleeping quarters either. It was dark, but dim light bulbs guided me on my way.

Valee was a traditional woman with high moral values. She had grown up with loving and caring parents who believed in education and that a life with a profession would result in less mistakes made and more prosperity; not necessarily to become wealthy, but to live with a dignity of one's own making. I had felt fortunate to have her as my possible future life partner, but now I was not sure, it was no longer my decision, it was hers. She would have to decide whether to keep me or not. I felt no shame in letting the tears drop; I sat on a rotten stump on the side of the road and cried, carelessly as if they were ants crawling down my nose, though I couldn't see them in the dark.

I heard a dog barking in the distance. The sound reminded me of my past, when I was still living in the village and every time the dogs barked it meant a stranger was coming. At the moment, there was no such stranger coming, we were all strangers to one another; the people living in the long huts had come from different towns, villages and provinces of Laos. Now we were living in the same village, or rather camp. We had become acquainted, and there were no strangers to the dogs in my mind. I walked toward the barking, and as I got closer, it increased in volume and urgency, as though the dog were about to bite someone. When I got closer, the dog ran away, still barking. I ignored it and was walking toward the narrow and shallow ditch when I heard someone cry out to my right, and I turned and rushed over, stumbling in the dark.

"Help me!" cried a woman. I crouched down, but it was difficult to see as I reached my hand toward her. She couldn't stand by herself. As I tried to help her up, I felt the cool blood, so I pulled her up and hoisted her onto my back to carry her to Valee. The dog kept barking, and followed us for several hundred feet before stopping. I had to bang hard on Valee's door. "Open the door, V, it is an emergency!" She opened the door wearing her pyjamas, and poked her head out. "Drunk," she muttered, and went back inside to get the lamp. When she held it up, she saw us.

"Sky lightning!" she said. I laid the woman down on the dirt floor and Valee ran to the clinic to get a bottle of alcohol and a pair of scissors. She told me to hold the woman's hand while she cleaned her face. There was a large cut across her forehead that was still bleeding, and Valee wrapped a bandage around her head. As she continued her examination, she discovered that a few of the woman's teeth were loose. As she moved downward on her body, she was pleased to discover that there were no cuts anywhere else, just some bruises. Valee went back to the clinic again and brought back a set of clothes. We took off the woman's blood-soaked clothes and cleaned her up before Valee put the fresh clothes on her. There was a pile of clothing in a room beside the clinic which had been donated by charities around the world; churches, refugee sponsors and private donations all sent them to the camp administration for those who needed them.

After we had dressed the woman, we washed our hands with water from the plastic container by the door. "Thank you," I said to Valee and began to walk away. "Where are you going to sleep tonight?" she asked. "I'm not sure, maybe in my own room." She held the door open.

"You're not going to leave this injured woman here alone with me, are you?"I went back in. The woman started crying and complaining about the pain, so Valee gave her an aspirin. Valee tossed me a blanket and then went to sleep. I slept beside the woman on the dirt floor, hoping that Valee would call to me to come to bed, but she never did. The room was dark, and when I rolled myself onto my side my back touched the woman's arm. She pressed her front against my back and put her arm around my waist.

"Thank you for helping," she said, still sobbing. I waited for her to speak or explain, but there were no more words. I knew Valee was not sleeping either. I felt as though we were far away from each other, our words could not make us agree on our personal doubts: she thought that I still hoped to get back to Nang Ya, but while I still had compassion for Nang Ya and missed her, I had never thought of going back to her.

Some hours later the woman pushed on my back and asked if she could wash herself. She said she felt something coming out of her vagina and had pain running through her upper legs. I woke Valee up to help her. Valee asked me to hold up the lamp as she pulled up the woman's sarong. She was bleeding, so Valee laid her back down and checked to see if she was cut inside. She told me to lower the light so that she could see what was wrong.

She could not see anything, but cleaned the blood away and put a towel between the woman's legs, telling her to keep it there through the night. She told her to let her know if there was pain again.

I sat beside the woman. A few minutes after she had gone to bed, Valee came back and sat beside me in the dark. The woman was silent. Valee took my hand and we lay down. "How did you find her?"

"In the ditch."

"What made you go there?"

"You don't need to ask that question," I said. "Why not?"

"Because it doesn't make sense.

"It makes sense to me."

"Do you want me to leave?"

"That is not what I wanted to know, I wanted to know why you went there?"

"I heard a dog barking, an unusual bark."

"How do you know usual from unusual, I thought that when a dog is barking, it's just barking?"

"Yes it is, but unusual barking is when there is something about the speed that makes it sound as if the dog would like to bite. Why are you talking to me like an interrogator?"

"Because I am!" I was silent, not trying argue anymore until she changed her questions to the fact that I was about to go and visit Nang Ya in prison, and had not stopped going to do so.

"After she was arrested, it should have put her out of our concern, Bo, all the police and human rights representatives would need or want is to come and ask you questions during the investigation, you don't need to go to the prison if you don't want to," she explained. "I know," I said. "You know what? What the fuck is it that you know?!"

I did not know how to explain how I felt. I hoped she would understand and drop the fight, but she continued, like someone who has no knowledge of anything. "I know I don't have to visit her, but it was you idea to help protect my life by living in hiding then eventually asking her to sign the papers so I could be free."

"Oh, be free of what? Did you have a secret marriage to her that I didn't know about?"

"No! Please don't think like that, Valee, what is wrong with you?" She stopped yelling. I turned to her, and put my arm around her shoulder and my left leg on top of her. "I hope that by now you know that we should get married," she said. She kept saying that she wanted to be sure I was ready and that there was no one else on my mind that would make me doubt that. Before I could answer the woman called out to us. "I am sorry if I am causing you trouble," she said. "Not at all," I replied.

Valee went over to the woman and explained that our argument was nothing to do with her being in the room. She told her that tomorrow we would take her to the office and she would have to explain everything to the guards and they would find out who was responsible for her injuries. We went to sleep and the next morning the woman had disappeared without a trace. Valee wrote a report anyway and gave it to Mr. Boun Young the next day.

Chapter 19

Valee's report sheet read: At around nine o'clock on November 17, 1979, Bo brought a woman of about 23 years to my sleeping quarters. She had a cut on her forehead, bruises on her upper legs and right side, two missing teeth and bleeding from her vagina. Her clothes were soaked with blood and she was in great pain, crying through most of the night she stayed in my room. I bathed her and gave her fresh clothing and painkillers. I waited to speak to her until the morning, but when I awoke, she was gone. My assumption is that she was raped by one or more men. Valee SavannaVong, nurse at clinic #21, Nong Khai Refugee Camp.

When the director had finished examining Valee's report the following morning, he called both of us into his office for questions. We didn't hear anything from him for two weeks, though Valee and I were curious about the woman. I decided to go and see the director to learn more about the matter. When I suggested that the night I found the woman I had no intention of going there and rescuing her, nothing of the sort, he smiled and told me that I had done the right thing by helping her. Then, he told me I should keep my mouth shut and not reveal the woman's situation.

"There were a number of things about the victim you helped," he started. "She was working as a prostitute in one of the brothels in Nong Khai, and she heard that her parents had escaped from Laos and were coming to the camp looking for her, and she was happy to be going to join them. She ran away from the brothel and came back to the camp, but there she continued having sex for money without paying the pimp, lying to him that she was no longer selling her body, but they found out that she was offering her services in the camp. She was offering herself anywhere that was available, such as out in the pasture by the camp. The brothel sent three men out to rape her, not to get money from her, but to teach her a lesson, so that she wouldn't speak out in public, not to foreigners, not to aid-workers, not to journalists, observers of refugees or tourists, or she would be killed.

Listening to the director's warning, I thought of my own case. Learning to be silent was important in order to stay safe in the camp, at least until we finally left. I left the office and went to the clinic. Valee said she would come and see me that evening, so I left for work. When Valee came to see me that evening, I had thought I would tell her about the business with the woman, but before I could speak she brought the conversation around to Nang Ya. "When are you going to see her next?"

"See who?" I asked, making sure of whom she was talking about. "See your girlfriend."

"You are my girlfriend," I said. "Thank you, but I mean the one who is in prison."

"I would rather you not talk about her; I would like you to talk about us."

"I will talk about us only when you stop seeing her."

"There is nothing to say, Valee," I replied. "Each time I see her in prison, she is sitting on the other side of a thick glass window."

"That is what I mean, words and mind are more important than touch, you know."

I was trying to find the moment to tell her what the director had told me about the woman. I had to wait until later, when she had verbally harassed me enough that I judged she was satisfied with my acceptance of her scolding and my apologies. "That is terrible, where is she now?" she asked after I had finished. "I don't know," I said. "The director told me to keep my mouth shut. From now on, I think we both have to forget about her and never talk about it anymore."

"But I'm still going to talk about Nang Ya," she said, finally in a half-joking mood, but still irritating me with her insistence. She was so stubborn and ignorant, but somehow sweet at the same time. "But can I still sleep with you?" I asked lightly. "You will have to wait," she said. "I have to go; I will see you tomorrow after work." She left the room and gradually the blue sky darkened. I went for a shower, and when I got back, Vanna was at my door shouting at me to come over to her side for supper. I told her I wasn't very hungry, but she insisted I come anyway and have a drink with Seath. The rice was still warm and the fish smelled excellent; it had been a long time since I had eaten traditional Lao cooking. Seath handed me a tiny cup of homemade whisky. "I can't empty it in one shot," I confessed. "Bring him a cup of water," he asked his wife, so that I would have something to drink after the whisky.

The darkness had reached its deepest point and the whole camp returned to silence. Seath crawled to bed. The lamp dimmed as it gradually ran out of kerosene. The colder air came out to meet us once in a while. Vanna was dressed in a blue-and-white-striped dress with a short-sleeved shirt through which I could see her white bra and erect breasts. "It has been over a year now since our son died, and Seath never sleeps with me," she said. "He doesn't even lay his eyes on me. Long before we got married when we were still living in Laos, he used to take me to his parents rice paddy. When the rain came we would go in and stay in the hut for hours until the rain stopped. He was so passionate with me then. Now I feel ugly and lonely," she said. "I hope that my husband still loves me and thinks I am worthy."

I was a bit surprised that she was speaking to me of her personal feelings. It was interesting to me, though, that the couple was in their mid-forties, and the husband was already losing sexual interest. After we had been silent a moment, a terrible snore came from Seath. The sounds he made were like pigs crying, among other animals. "I got jealous the other night, hearing you and Valee making love in your room," she confessed. At that point, I felt very uncomfortable and embarrassed.

"I think I should go," I told her. She started sobbing."I'm sorry; please don't get the wrong idea," she said, hugging me tightly, "Good night." I felt for Vanna—for her sexual desire and need for love. I thought that maybe it was partly due to the fact that she did not do enough physical activity and had too much free time.

I went and lay on my bed with my eyes open for a long time. I turned Valee's words over and over in my mind, and then thought again of the look she had given me when she said "You will have to wait." How much longer would I have to wait? She knew of my desire for her, but was ignoring it. She seemed even to be enjoying the fact that I was suffering by being deprived of her, but I could not understand why she would do that.

Before I went to work the next morning, I went to see her. She was taking a shower, and when she returned she was drying herself with a white towel and carrying soap and shampoo. "Isn't your truck arriving?" she asked. "They will wait."

"I told you I would see you this evening."

"I know, I just wanted to see you before work."

"I'm still the same," she joked, and went inside. "See you tonight," I shouted, not going in.

November was a dry season. There was a little cold air in the evening and early morning, but during the day it was not much different from May to September, which were filled with heat and rain. Most of the time, the rain doesn't help cool things down, in many cases it even makes it worse with the humidity. But this morning was fair, not too hot. We rolled up our truck windows all the way from the camp to Nong Khai. I asked Mr. Broman if he could help me keep secret what we did in town, especially my visits to Nang Ya in prison. He then asked if what I was saying concerned public or private secrets. When I said private, a big smile came to his face and he slapped me on the back and before I could explain, he spoke.

"I know what you mean! I know what it is to be a man; we all have our dirty secrets, no matter what culture we come from."

"How do you know what I was going to say?"

"I've been there before you."

"I don't think it is the same."

"Not the situation, but the feeling." He said. "Go on."

"Well, my current girlfriend is very jealous, she always picks a fight when she knows I am going to visit the prison," I told him. "OK, that's simple: don't tell her."

"That was what I meant."

"Besides, we have asked you to go and see Nang Ya. Personally, do you want to see her?

"Yes."

"Good. It is very important to Nang Ya, you know, she has no one there except police, lawyers, and other professionals. They just go and see her for reasons related to the case, but you are the only other one. We need you to be a witness, or to get information from her, but you are also her good friend."

"And I know she is always happy to see me," I said. "I know," he said, "your presence means a great deal to her." He looked at me in the eye. "Everything will work out, my friend." This was his catch-phrase, he repeated it often.

I felt then that I had made a terrible deal with him to lie to Valee each time I visited Nang Ya. In the Buddhist tradition, lying to a loved one is a sin. However, in the social norm, lying to someone to avoid conflict is clever. What made it different was that I was lying to Valee, the woman I planned to spend the rest of my life with, for Nang Ya, with whom I had a strong past, and had a lot of heartfelt experiences, but life had to go on.

"I am a liar," I said to myself. My mother would never have approved of this. Before we approached the warehouse, Mr. Broman suddenly said Bo!" I turned to him and he said "How come you always call me Mr. Broman, and sometimes just Broman? You know, Broman is my last name, and you can call my father Mr. Broman if he is here, my name is Larry."

"I am sorry," I said. "You don't need to apologise, it's just to make things easier. Hi! My name is Larry, Larry Broman, and then you're supposed to say, Hi! My name is Bond, James Bond!" We both laughed hard before changing the subject.

"Have you heard the song 'Let it be?'" Larry asked. "What is it?"

"You know that song by The Beatles? I'm not sure of the name of the singer, but I'm sure it was one of the Beatles…" He started singing it then. "What is it about?" I interrupted. "Well, you know, let things be the way they are," he said.

When I first met him, I didn't think he would allow this kind of casual talk and humour between us. I had seen him as a boss and myself as an employee, and I felt that bosses and employees had a special kind of relationship, with no jokes or signs of real human nature, but what was most important to me was that he was a white man who had at one time been a conqueror of the world, and was even now involved with charity work with the poor and vulnerable. Now I had learned that he was just another human being, just Larry, my friend, who had a story to tell.

At lunch we ate at a stand beside the road. Larry looked at the girl who was sitting under a red and white umbrella beside us chopping the papaya. “It is amazing how she does it,” he exclaimed. While waiting for our meal, and having nothing to say, I watched the woman cooking our fish, turning it over the charcoal stove, making sure it was well-cooked. The oil from the fish dripped down onto the hot burning coals below, making smoke stream up thickly and sending its aroma into the air, which made me even hungrier and my mouth began to water.

We ate. Our thoughts since we had sat down at the stand had been only of that moment, and while waiting neither of us had felt like talking much, we just watched the people around us and made comments. It was once we began to eat that we really talked. Larry looked at me. “Don’t you want to know Larry’s story?”

“Yes sir. Not necessarily the personal things, but at least where you grew up.”

He thought for a while and then smiled, still chewing, and signalled to me with his finger to wait a moment. Once he had swallowed he told me he was born in 1949 in a small town about 100 kilometres south of Sydney, in Australia. He stayed in the country until he graduated from university, at which point he went with his girlfriend at the time to India. They visited the slums, where people were living in cardboard boxes. He stayed there for six weeks, and each day he saw how the people struggled not only to find ways to make a living, but they also suffered police brutality. The police would not only arrest people breaking the law by stealing or sleeping in public spaces but would also beat them with their batons and force them to pay the police. Larry found it inhuman, but had no power or capacity to help with the unjust treatment of the powerless.

When he returned to Australia that year, he told his girlfriend that he wanted to postpone their marriage and enrolled for Graduate studies in Sociology. Two months into the semester, his girlfriend left him to marry someone else, and Larry had no plans for a family. Shortly after, he dropped out of university. "Australia is a fine country," he said, "One has the opportunity to choose a future and live as he desires. In my lifetime, I have never experienced war. I left my home, neither for reasons of safety or politics, but because I had the choice to do so."

He didn't tell me of his childhood years, what was what interested me most. However, I found it interesting that he had taken social problems personally, and had decided to spend his life helping the needy people of the world. I guessed that he must be learning a great deal in his field work, maybe even more than he would have learned by studying the theory. For some reason, that day we talked all day, which made me worry less about my situation.

After Larry dropped me off that afternoon, I went straight to the shower. When I returned, Valee was at the door, smiling. "How was your day?" she asked. "Good!"

"Is this for real?" I asked, "Are you asking me out?"

"Shut up!" she cracked back. We went for a walk all the way across the camp by the narrow short-cut streets. There were children spraying each other with water along our way, and some women were walking behind us wearing mini-skirts. I turned my head from time to time, until Valee stopped walking and turned to face me.

"Do you find her attractive?"

"She is striking," I said. "She is good-looking." I got the feeling that my behaviour, looking at another woman, made Valee mad. She looked me in the eye. "Don't you want to know what I have been doing today?" I hadn't thought much about the details of her day, and although it was always a pleasure to hear about what she had done, I didn't think I would have to ask. "What were you doing?"

"It was not a good day for me. I saw a child die. Her mother brought her into the clinic early this morning, telling us that she had been complaining of stomach pain, shortness of breath and dizziness. I sent my niece to get the doctor right away, and when he arrived the child stopped breathing. The death itself did not make me emotional; it was the mother's mourning. She was losing it, crying and slamming her face against the wall."

I saw tears dripping from her eyelids. "Do you want to go back?"

"No, no! It's ok, I just wanted to talk!" When we reached the east edge of the camp, Valee looked into my eyes again. "Hold me," she told me. When I did hold her, she started to kiss me hard. We went back to my room. Vanna was at the door holding a tray with supper. When she saw I had company, she smiled to both of us, handed me the tray and left. I put the tray on my bed and took Valee's hand, guiding her out. "Why?" she asked. "Well, Vanna is a nosy woman. I don't want us to do anything in there anymore."

"Did she hear us last time?"

"I think so."

Instead of getting upset, Valee laughed so hard that it made me laugh too, not about Vanna but about Valee's reaction to the matter. "What an animal she is, spying on us!" she said. I considered telling her about my discussion with Vanna, but did not want to start a fight. We walked back across the camp, as darkness emerged. We wandered without destination, just enjoying each other's company and touch. Once in a while we would stop and Valee would kiss me, deeply. When we approached the school, she stopped again. I took her hand and led her inside.

When she leaned her back against the long table, I discovered that underneath her jogging pants, she had nothing on, or under her tee-shirt. I pulled the shirt up as far as her chin. She didn't like that and pulled it off over her head. I pulled her jogging pants off completely, and she started crying out with excitement, letting the sound go with unlimited passion, the free spirit of lovemaking. I walked back to her place. I was feeling less stressed, as once again Valee and I had not had a fight that day.

Chapter 20

I woke up that Monday morning with excitement mixed with other feelings. Vanna shouted to remind me about my appointment. As we knew, for some reason the prison director was allowing me to visit Nang Ya at ten o'clock, like the last time. Each time I was allowed to see her, I hoped that she would have a nice long note for me.

I wanted to see her to hear about what she had done for the governor in all those months before she had been arrested. I didn't bother with my morning meal, so later on the road to the prison, my stomach started singing all along the way. At first Larry ignored the noise, but when the growling became more frequent, he asked if I wanted to eat something. I told him that I didn't want to be late, and he nodded.

When we arrived at the prison, the warden seemed to know us as well, and did not ask our names as he had done the first time, simply opened the gate and let us in. Larry returned outside, he told me later that while he waited, he had read the newspaper, an article about a thirty-three year old man who was swimming from Laos with his eight-year-old daughter on his back, and when they were in the middle of the Mekong they were shot by Lao communist police officers. Stories like this were a commonly heard, sometimes being covered by the media, but most often being spread by word of mouth. The shooting and killing of civilians was not necessary, a Lao communist police officer had said, sometimes it was the Thai police who did it as well.

When I saw Nang Ya walking toward me through the sheet of glass, she looked different. The shape of her face had changed, she was gaining weight, which struck me, because one would think that under the difficult circumstances, she might be eating and sleeping less, but the opposite must have been true. Her face was more rounded and her fingers were fleshier, and her breasts were like those of a pregnant woman, large and erect, though they were not very visible through her black prison uniform, which was two sizes too big.

I noticed for the first time that a prison official was not far from Nang Ya: she was seated at the end of the room on the left, watching us talking. Through the glass, I could only see her from her waist down, but I could see her baton, which nearly reached the floor where she sat. Nang Ya looked at her once in a while, which I found annoying, as I would sit in silence waiting for her attention to come back to me. I had expected that Nang Ya would ask something about how long she would have to wait for a trial, but I saw that she had no intention of doing so, nor did she seem to care about getting out of prison. Her air of normalcy was apparent; she did not seem frightened or sad, but did not laugh often either.

In her note she had written: "I have met a new friend, she told me how to avoid being beaten—to shave my head, get fat, always look up at the ceiling when walking in the corridor, and never say yes, to say only "haha" but looking straight into the person's eyes when talking to them. That is the norm here." The woman, Nang Ya's new friend, had been arrested for first degree murder, as she was accused of killing her husband's mistress' boyfriend. The woman told Nang Ya that one night her husband took her to the country, almost an hour's drive from Nong Khai, telling her that they were going to visit a friend with whom he had worked at the fish-sauce factory for more than ten years.

When they arrived at the house, however, they saw a dim light in the living room and a motorcycle parked under the house. As they walked up, they saw a woman seated on the floor wearing a traditional Thai sarong and the man leaning his back against the straw mattress as they talked and laughed. As they approached, the man sat up, looking very surprised when her husband aimed his handgun at him and fired two shots, killing him instantly. Her husband then handed her the gun and took her to the police station, where she was immediately arrested, and once in prison, she survived by learning how to be a good listener to the other prisoners.

"She said that almost all the woman prisoners wanted to tell her their stories, but to this day she never knows if they are true, or if the women are just making up something to talk about," Nang Ya said on the last page of her note. It was hard to tell whether the stories could be true or not, as generally they were criminals. The suspects therefore had a desire to explain their crime and the circumstances, some of which were very complicated, and some wanted to explain the injustices of the legal system, which I knew of from my other experiences with law-breakers.

After finishing talking about her new friend, Nang Ya turned back to her own situation. Back to the day the governor came to the school and took her to town. He had brought her to the restaurant, and afterward, he took her to the bungalow and they had sex. Before he sent her back, he told her that if she even mentioned their relationship to me, I would be killed and she would be sent to be a cheap prostitute in Bangkok or be killed herself and that he would put our names on a watch-list for communist spies that were a threat to Thailand security in order to justify the killings. I would simply suddenly disappear without a trace, as had happened to many other people he didn't like.

"I am now a stray dog, Bo, but I am glad that you are alive," she said, without looking in my eyes. Up to this point, her explanation had made me jealous that she had had sex with that tyrant, but now I was angry. "What happened after you went to see me in the camp and returned to him the next day?"

"He sent his bodyguards to you, and I was so frightened. I had no chance to return, but I missed you terribly. I paid five hundred Baht to the guard and agreed to have sex with him afterward. I won a bit of control for that, you know."

"How so?"

"Because by having sex with him, if he turned me down, I could tell the governor, so he was clever enough to help me when I needed him, until the last time, when he said he didn't want to take any more chances, though he remained respectful of me."

"How did the governor treat you then?"

"By nature he was very polite, a father-figure of sorts. He told me many times that I reminded him of the first girlfriend he had in college. He said he never had the chance to have sex with her, but had never forgotten her, and when he returned from studying in the United States, she had married someone else. His parents had arranged his own marriage, and some fifteen years later he became governor, but felt that his personal life had become rotten, so he would use the power he had in order to have me," she said. "He treated me with great respect as a woman, but his kindness and respectfulness only lasted a few months before he told me to bring more girls to work for his family. He became rude to me, always shouting, and told me that what he did was for my own good. He also only had sex with me on the weekends, where before it was three to five times a week."

It struck me that she spoke openly and without hesitation about the situation to try and make me jealous. Afterwards, I realized that she was simply hoping that I would come up with a new idea. It was not a regular sort of conversation or a series of questions and answers, she was simply reliving the time she spent as the governor's mistress. Each day, she would go into the camp with the driver and speak to the girls she found through the salons, offering them money for consensual sex. In the following days, she would send the driver to pick them up and bring them to her bungalow. She would then explain the process to them, and about how they would each be sent to a different "home:" Sweet Home, Banana Bush Home, Haven Home, Sunlight Home, Lover's Home, Old Man's Dream Home, and others. All these homes belonged to the same owner, the "Lesy Highness," which means White Saint. Even during the federal police investigation later, the media did not report on or clarify who this brothel owner was, and no indication was given that Lesy Highness even existed. The name, however, was a legendary one used in twelfth century myths.

The character of the governor was, in many respects, very generous. He had supported many charities even though he was never personally involved. He would send money and materials into the camp and to victims of natural disasters around the country. She said, however, that she never knew or understood his secret life, the necessity for business or other reasons of killing civilians and the criminal activities, and his attitude in threatening to kill me if she spoke out about their sexual relationship. These final words spoken, Nang Ya said that the food in the prison was excellent. She ate three full meals per day, which were made up of a variety of things like beef, fish, pork, and chicken; and was sent to work mostly on fruit farms.

She said it was a different life, but that there was never a minute where she was not thinking of me.

She walked back to the cell accompanied by two guards. I wasn't sure where the other guard had come from. As she turned into the hallway where the cells were from the main corridor, I realized that she was crying. I waited until she had disappeared from sight, and then the guard tapped me on the shoulder and told me to stand up. He opened the gate behind me and sent me back to the waiting room.

I remember that then, before she walked back to her cell, her attention was no longer on me, but elsewhere. I wasn't sure what to make of what she had said, as she continued asking about something else. What she had told me before leaving now returned to me: "I am done with you, I am sorry." She had cried afterward. In my mind, I wondered if it was the reality if what we were facing that made her talk like that: she was in prison; I was on the witness protection list. Our hope of being reunited was blocked. In prison they keep prisoners without trial for a long time, some never even made it to the court, but were somehow still convicted.

Larry, was nowhere in sight, so I walked outside. I found him in the truck re-arranging the paperwork. The glare of the late morning sun hit me in the eyes as though someone was shining a flashlight into them. When Larry turned the truck westward, the light was no longer in our faces, but the heat remained. Larry always wore sunglasses when he was driving, and whenever he looked at me, the brown lenses with his open eyes behind them looked like coiled snakes."Oooh, that's scary," I said.

"Do I look like a boogie-man?" he asked. I didn't know what that meant, so he explained and when he had finished, I said without thinking, "Let's hope that neither of us ever has to become a boogie-man."

Chapter 21

There are some things that I never thought would affect my mental health. A few days after I visited Nang Ya for the second time, I was struck by an emotional downfall. I cried most of the time when I was alone; there was all kinds of information coming into my mind, I thought about her constantly, about the kindness and softness we felt when we were together and our strong compassion for one another, and they way she had once asked me if some day I would marry her. I began to realize that for the many months since the day she had left me, I had been angry and stressed about the unknown cause that had influenced her decision. In addition, I was drawn to hateful thoughts, hating her behavior and the fact that I could not trust her, her simple mindset and the way she had walked away without much explanation, leaving me and continuing to lie about all those activities in town, the months she had left me to suffer until I ran out of patience and rationalization of her actions and gave up out of spite.

The change in my perception came soon after I left the prison. Until she revealed her relationship with the governor, I had never thought that this kind of thing would happen in real life. There were only the legendary tales about people having to give up their ordinary lived in order to protect those that they loved. Most of the tales had to do with political rivalry, but she had become a stray to keep me alive.

A day after her arrest they had brought her into a larger room with many other prisoners. All of them, except for her, were Thai. She said they had screamed when they saw her and asked her what she had done. She told them that she killed a rapist, and they made a lot of noises for some time. Some made chimpanzee noises, encouraging her bravery. At nightfall, many of them wanted to show her their prisoners' attitude, appearing over-confident, swearing, and generally acting fearless and influential, but they were also sharing their personal stories and of what they had done. That first night she was like a new wolf in a pack, with every other wolf sniffing to get a sense of who she was.

As she slept, she felt bugs crawling over her face, legs and arms. The next day, she changed from the sarong she had been wearing to long jeans, to protect her from the bugs, until she was given her prison uniform. Later that evening, however, she felt something very prickly on her nose and when she put her hand to her face, she found a millipede, about to crawl into her nose. She screamed and took the millipede off, throwing it away from her, but the stupid thing landed on another woman's head and she screamed as well. After the guard came to turn out the light, Nang Ya apologized to the woman, but she thought that she had done it on purpose and beat her until she bled. One of the women who would later become Nang Ya's friend would tell her that night that from then on she would need to have an over-confident attitude.

Some days later, Nang Ya would be given a uniform and was put into a cell by herself where she slept on a bad with one side screwed to the wall. There were a couple of other pieces of furniture, a thin brown metal desk and a matching chair, and a toilet with neither a seat nor a flush handle. A small bucket was provided to fill with water to pour into the toilet to flush it. There was a rusted tap coming out of the wall, but the long water-pipe was nowhere to be seen. She told me later that the cell was her last home, neither she nor I knew that it would be the home where she would know the best living conditions she had seen outside her family, or that she would one day return to be reunited with real society. In our thoughts and imagination, there still remained the hope that she could one day be free, but under the circumstances, what society would accept a criminal into its midst, even the country where she always wanted to live, in Canada, specifically Quebec? It would be a miracle if it came to be.

Alone on my day off, I wandered into a nearby dark forest which was part of the underdeveloped area of Thailand. The trees were mostly Tama rang trees about thirty to fifty feet high and very clear of branches. The leaves are smaller than a fingernail, but grew in bunches which made them look larger. The bunches were a few inches apart and among them hung brown-looking fruit.

Beneath the Tama rang trees was tall grass and a small pile of bamboo left over from cattle being fed. The small pathway snaked through the forest made of softened ground that turned to mud in the rainy season and became dry and dusty in the dry season. The dust coated the leaves alongside the path as animals walked on it. My feet weren't powerful enough to raise dust, but my footprints remained as I walked along. The smell of animal urine was unavoidable, but the breeze making its way through the trees encouraged me to carry on walking. I had no ultimate goal in mind, but kept walking, following my instinct that there might be another road ahead.

I stopped walking in a clearing. I was feeling very sad inside and looked up without any intensity at the aggressive clouds above. They were streaming out from one great chunk of cloud, trailing away to the west and disappearing. Within a minute or so, the whole big chunk of cloud had vanished, gone to nowhere, but I stood where I had stopped. Then I stepped into the forest again, continuing on the same path, never knowing where it would end, waiting for another clearing. When my legs began shaking and my heartbeat began to slow, it convinced me to sit down for a while.

I sat on a rotten stump, looking out over the Tama rang trees. The wind pushed them, and they bowed in whichever direction the wind blew them before the whole body of each tree swung back and forth. I watched this happen for an hour, sitting there. Once again, I heard Nang Ya's voice: "I love you. If I can do anything to make you happy that will be the day." I lay back on the ground, looking up to the clouds again. My mouth was salty as I thought back to the day we had met two years ago. "When did you get here?" she asked. "This morning."

"Did you escape alone?"

"Yes. You?"

"With my two friends, but they are not with me; one vanished while we were swimming and the other two days after."

Then, my thoughts turned to a week later, when we had met again. "You are very kind, how come you didn't bring your girlfriend with you?"

"She died while we were in school up north."

"I am sorry. Do you still love her?"

"Always, but I have to move on with my life and hope one day someone will come along and I will love her even more."

"Do you mean her or the new one?"

"The new one, of course." She smiled then, and began to laugh, and I laughed too. "Have you ever thought about marriage?"

"All the time, but I always thought it would be after I completed my Masters degree."

"Do you think you will ever get the chance to go back to school?"

"Yes, but not in Thailand, though."

"Where would it be?"

"In North America."

"How about in European countries?"

"Maybe, but those would be my last resort."

"Why last?"

"I don't have enough knowledge to explain, it is just a feeling that I would have less chance of an opportunity to have a decent job or continue studying."

"What do you want to do if you get a chance to do graduate studies?"

"My greatest desire is to become a university professor, teaching sociology, culture in particular."

I began to feel cold and realized that what had been coming into my head for the last little while wasn't real. The voice in my head was only my emotional attachment to Nang Ya, who I knew wouldn't have the opportunity to meet me in a place where we could kiss, hug, touch, and make love in that manner. But there was hollowness in that I could never understand where the sadness in my body came from. Nang Ya's words kept coming back into my head: "I went with him to save your life, Bo. As I stood up and walked back to the camp, the darkness arrived.

Walking in the dark, I realized memories of my relationship with Nang Ya had returned and were torturing me. My thoughts often strayed and to unrelated things without my intention. Focusing on staying in touch with the camp administrators and foreign immigration officers, it made me more curious about what Nang Ya had said about prostitute recruitment. It was unclear to me from her description whether the governor was the head of this prostitution business or if he had been taking bribes from those involved with organized crime. The gentle being as she had described him was only his outward appearance; she hadn't gotten to tell me about his internal evil soul. I wondered too if he was a governor due to his political ideology and served the public as his title would have us believe, or if he used that title as a mass image to manipulate the law while blocking from the public view the exchange of millions of dollars with brother businesses. The governor, Vannaran, who I had met at the school with Nang Ya, seemed to have a shallow thinking capacity. I had noted the day I met him that when his entire team had shaken my hand, he hadn't, shooting me a dirty look instead. I would realize later that this was because of his desire for Nang Ya.

I had been having great difficulty in my mind as this whole matter left me with doubts. However, as we had continued our relationship, I had done my best to find a way to understand. It had never solved the problem, though. I was something of an obsessive person when I was younger; if someone touched someone I loved, I could never take her back afterward. However, at that time, I had done more rationalizing about it. As a matter of fact, Nang Ya had not gone looking for her new relationship, she had been drawn by circumstance, whatever that was, and always maintained her support and care for me. She returned often to the camp, and each time brought messages of love, food, books, and the time for long love-making.

Chapter 22

During her first trial at the court, Nang Ya had changed her personality. Wearing a blue vest with a white blouse underneath and a long blue skirt, her hair brushing her shoulders and subtle makeup, she looked like a professional banker, however she looked as though she did not know what to think. I found that she had difficulty communicating to her lawyer and reacting to the prosecutor, and even to the judge. I wasn't sure if she noticed that I was there observing the hearing. As the prosecutor questioned her, she smiled often. There was no jury, but three judges, clerks, guards, and others who looked like students.

"Did you kill the police officer?" the prosecutor asked. "I'm not sure."

"Yes or no, did you kill the police officer?"

"I said I wasn't sure, I never learned how to shoot a gun."

"But how was it then that the gun shot the police officer in his mouth."

"I don't know."

"Did you touch the gun?"

"Yes."

"Why?"

"Because he asked me to hold it just for fun, that's all I can remember. He warned me not to put my finger on the trigger."

The examination went on for forty five minutes. Afterward, one of the guards took her arm in the witness box and led her out of the courtroom. I remembered then a conversation I had with Mr. Boun Young when he had told me something about Thai law. He said that the death penalty was practiced there, but that even the most serious cases involving drugs and murder had to clearly determine guilt on the basis of evidence. Therefore, Nang Ya's case might not qualify for a death sentence, and besides, since she was not a Thai citizen, it might be argued that police brutality or abuse of human rights was involved in taking a young woman from a UN camp. It could also be argued that it had been an accident. Boun Young had also mentioned an incident with an Indian who was working for the UN in Thailand, who might be interested in defending Nang Ya. He told me to stay calm, since thinking about a problem is not what created it, the problem had come about when we had left our home, but we were in it now. He said he thought that Nang Ya was aware that she was in the problem, and that either she or we would have to deal with it, but that we shouldn't make ourselves sick thinking about it. He suggested that it might have been someone else who had used Nang Ya in the hotel that day with the officer, that someone else had killed him and then put him there to blame it on her. I hoped that there was a way to help her get out of jail. If someone could bring the Indian lawyer to help defend her, it would surely impact in a good way, though it was already a specialized Thai lawyer representing her. He seemed to just collect information and present her; he showed no motivation to protect her with any sort of strong argument.

He had her there in court for no reason other than to ask questions of when needed. At the same time, I wasn't sure the UN representatives were putting that much effort into her case, as there were many other refugees with greater problems in other places. We were important to ourselves as human beings, and had feelings and thoughts, and a desire for good lives, but we were not well-known in the world. We did not have the status of great importance to our country, like Albert Einstein or Bruce Lee. We were poor refugees. The lawyer's opinion must have made sense to him, but there is no historical evidence that even the Indian lawyer could perform miracles.

In the truck, Larry started the engine and put his hand on my chest. "Be calm, buddy," he said and looked at me. I smiled. "I'm ok." We arrived at the camp at 4 pm and he dropped me off at the side gate. I stepped out and was about to shut the door, but he held it open.

"Remember, don't be sad, huh? Tell Valee I said hi." I bit my lip and walked past the gate. The guard waved at me. I thought that Valee would probably already have left the clinic, but I stopped by there to be sure. She was just about to leave, but had stopped to talk to a woman who had one eye covered with a white patch. Both of them looked up as I walked in.

"Hi! Are you coming to my place tonight?" I asked "I'm not sure," she said, and waved me away, glancing at the other woman. As I walked away, they continued talking. I hoped that she would come over. Vanna was making a bamboo soup. The fire was like a burning forest in her little kitchen. She was sweating like a galloping pony.

"Go and change, supper will be ready soon." It wasn't an invitation, Vanna was like family now. I ate at her place every day, and gave her three quarters of my supplies, saving just a bit to share with Valee, as sometimes we cooked together. I found it was reasonable: rice, cooking oil, sometimes meat and vegetables and salt. After supper, Seath went to see the cock-fight, so Vanna and I went to sit outside the hut to talk. She continued where we had left off the last time, talking about their relationship. She said that Seath is now more likely to leave her on her own as he goes off to drink and gamble and hang out with his friends, friends that he knew from his old country. Vanna seemed frustrated by her husband's behavior and with her own loneliness, often weeping as she spoke. I had great respect for her maturity, she often had sensible advice.

When we broke off our conversation, the darkness emerged and the sky seemed to lower itself closer to us; the stars were not born until evening arrived. Then there were many of them, and to me it looked like the sky was moving up high away from us. I thought, if I were a counselor, a monk or a Catholic priest, something like that, I could be more useful to Vanna for her difficulties. However, I was only a person who could talk to her, well enough only to be able to respond to her questions, though sometimes I doubted that what I had said was suitable to the matter at hand. I wished I had known more about psychology or had enough knowledge of the Buddhist methodology to be able to calm the mind in times of distress such as this one. Anyway, when someone is sad, they need some affection, and if they cannot get it from a loved one, they look for it from an acquaintance.

Vanna put her arms around my neck and continued mumbling, kissing my cheek from time to time. I was seven or eight years older than her dead son, she might think about him or miss him a great deal, and I thought maybe she was reflecting this on me. Her affectionate behavior was somehow more than the usual sort which occurred between adults of different genders. She was always wearng Tang top to keep her cool.

When Valee arrived, I stood up, and Vanna asked me to pull her hand up. I did, and she and Valee stood chatting while I stepped back into our room and took a seat. It was silent for a while, and after a few minutes I lit the lamp. Valee walked in and lifted up my t-shirt, sliding her hands over my belly and chest. As I pushed them away so I could stand up, she started to tickle me. I told her to stop the nonsense, but she carried on more aggressively. In return, I had no choice but to pin her down and start tickling her back. She laughed very loudly, screaming and begging me to stop. I did not stop. "You were asking for it!" I said. She rolled on top of me and started kissing me. I pushed her off. "It's enough," I told her. She stood up, fixing her clothes, and stepped back outside. After I had fixed my own clothes, I blew out the lamp and followed her outside. The crickets were everywhere, making the sounds of the night-life. As we walked to the new whiskey-stand, I heard many calls from people inviting us in for a drink. I waved to them.

"It is fine with me if you want to go in," Valee said. "No, I only go there if you're not with me."

"Why do you say that?"

"I say that because when you are not with me, I am sad and I need to drink."

"Good to know, but why do you have to be sad?"

"Just kidding."

"No, I'm serious, why?"

"I said, I am just kidding, it is no big deal, ok?"

"It is a big deal for me, why?" She walked ahead of me and then turned to face me, looking me in the eyes. I couldn't see her because of the darkness, but when we kept walking and passed a street-light, I saw that she was not smiling. "I'm very concerned about you, why would you say such a thing, that you are sad when I am not with you, you don't trust me?"

"It is not about trust; I just miss you, ok? If what I said made you uncomfortable, I'm sorry; I just want you to know that it doesn't mean anything. Come closer to me or you will step on a rat!" She held my arm.

We were silent for a while, until we reached the edge of the camp, near the football field. Then she began telling me about the woman. She had received 35 US dollars from her ex-boyfriend, who lived in Des Moines, Iowa. He had been there since 1976 and had a job in a factory that producing hospital supply, which gave him one of the higher salaries in manual labor work in the state and he wanted to send some money to help her in the camp. Her husband found out and told her to return the cheque. She went to Nong Khai with her friend and cashed it, and bought herself clothes instead. He got angry and swung his saddle at her, hitting her in the face. The metal pin on the saddle cut her eyelid and she went to the clinic. After she had been treated, she told Valee about her situation and asked for her advice. Valee apologized for her behavior earlier, making a joke that when I had gone to see her and she had said she wasn't sure if she would come and see me, that I should not have been confused [about whether she wanted to]. Accusations or misunderstandings were not the core of our relationship, it was the humor that we both wanted to bring up from our spontaneous feelings, and however, speaking without thinking created unpleasant feelings and forced us to question the matter. (She was still scared of the rats and clung to my arm) I found that after only a few minutes, Valee was calm and had forgotten her anger.

By then, we shouldn't have had anything against one another or been holding back any more feelings. But each day of our separation, during which we experienced different situations and other people's problems, which sometimes included ourselves. The lack of proper behavior and thinking before acting of this sort creates great negative impact on one's relationships. In order not to say more things to Valee in the case of something which I thought was not a major problem in our relationship, I usually just said I was sorry, which calmed the situation down. However, it was never guaranteed that I would not say something which would offend her or someone else I was talking to, it was just a perception, something that someone perceived and recalled as wrong. I found it to be much lacking in social engagement, and showing too much desire to one another.

Anyway, we continued walking and Valee took hold of my hand and swung my arm as a young child often does with their parent. We were not children and did not have our parents with us. At our age, the rich are still students living in their parents' houses and spending their money, but an average citizen our age has settled down to be parents of our own children. In many ways, however, our maturity was somehow mixed; as we discussed life in general and solved our problems and made mistakes and did what we had to do to prolong our relationship and come to a solid ground before becoming a couple. Here we no longer had parents or guidelines for our family plan; like young ponies, who, after stopping nursing, were disconnected. Some would stray, but others would stay with their owners and work in order to earn their protection. Unlike humans, they are protected by us, but who is protecting us?

That morning I had witnessed Nang Ya's first trial with a compassion for the young woman I had once felt passionate about. Only nine hours later, I was with a woman who had admitted that she loved me, and wanted to extend that love and affection to create a family. I no longer made my own judgments about whether or not to select the path and play the role, it is a form of nature, just as when the young pony becomes separated from its mother and does not have a foal of its own. We reached the north-east end of the camp and returned back to Valee's place.

The street was dark, and when I started down the narrow street to her place, I stepped into a pothole with my right foot, down into a pool of dark mud that smelled of pigs. Valee held my arm and we went to her room to get changed. I went to the shower stall to wash my foot, taking off my jeans and shoes to hold it up to the tap. It was quiet, nobody was there. I put my jeans on the floor and Valee came in and took hers off, leaning her back against the wall and drawing me into a passionate kiss. She would tell me later that she never used any birth control, since she wanted to get pregnant.

I hadn't thought of, nor planned on, starting a family. If Valee got pregnant and had a child, that would be it. I hadn't planned on starting a family while living in the middle of nowhere, but the family started me. I knew Nang Ya still had her pride, and even though we were still seeing each other, the personal bond was no longer as strong, as we knew both our worlds were falling apart. What she had been through as the governor made our lives fall into problems kept turning over endlessly in my mind, making it difficult to make decisions and often leading to fear.

Chapter 23

The governor's mansion is in the midst of a mango grove. It has two storage buildings with red roofs made out of clay. The exteriors are painted white and the window-frames are brown. Each room had an air-conditioner which extended about six inches from the side walls. There were no houses around it that were anything like it, not only in terms of size, but also style. The only one which came close was the imperial bank which stood on Main Street, but that was a commercial building, and did not compare to it in artistic creation. The mansion stood by itself some one thousand feet from the main road which snaked along the Mekong. Local residents called it a "giant cave" since only giant beings were allowed to visit, meaning people of high profile such as politicians, officers at the head of government or organized-crime bosses. The only lower people who were allowed to visit were the ones who worked there, however not his mistresses, since his wife resides there. The police who were selected to guard him were only the best, having been trained in the military of something of that sort.

Once, just to impress Nang Ya, the governor had driven her by his mansion so she would look at what he had before he took her back to the bungalow for sex, leaving her there for another day before he would pick her up again. For all the time before she was arrested, Nang Ya had been feeling ambivalent. She was living well, with good food, clothes and trips, and was gaining respect from the governor's people and the other sex workers. Her mental state, however, was suffering as she found herself in a storm of problems of self-identity, love and compassion caused by thinking of me daily. To avoid me being killed by her rapist, who was trying to silence her, she remained loyal to the governor.

Once in the hotel in Bangkok, Nang Ya asked the governor to be allowed to visit me after they returned to Nong Khai, and he hit her in the right ear with a rolled-up newspaper, then raped her repeatedly. In the morning, when the room-service man came to knock on the door, the governor opened the door and took the tray from him. He tried to put ice on Nang Ya's ear to make the bruise disappear. In the evening, when he had gone to the bar on the first floor, Nang Ya went to the restaurant downstairs to get some iced tea. The waitress asked her what she had done to her cheek and ear, and she said she had fallen in the shower. When the waitress asked if she would like her to get the doctor to check it, she said not to bother and went back to her room.

The forty-year-old woman reported the incident to the hotel manager and the next morning two members of the administration came and asked some questions. They were concerned for the safety and reputation of their business, and the questioning was part of their protocol. Before the questions got too detailed, the governor said he would pay the staff 500 bhat in Thai money not to bother him again. When he told them who he was, they were silent. Nang Ya kept telling the governor that she did not tell them anything about her injury, but when they returned to Nong Khai, he had sex with her repeatedly on the train and told her that if she told anyone, including his personal driver, about the incident, he would have her drowned in the Mekong. The next day, he had her go to the clinic and told her not to do anything for two weeks.

"My future was gone, and then I thought about you and cried for most of my two weeks off from recruiting innocent young girls for him," she said. She paused and then continued. "I died inside a long time ago, Bo, please forgive me if this hurts you."

Until now, without her diary, there was no chance that I could know her daily occupations. Knowing it created a greater sense of how vulnerable I was to the fact that my status was so low, and that I had ability to defend her or myself, we had no choice but to let the unknown torture us, mentally and physically. Since she was not allowed to have notebooks in prison, Nang Ya wrote her daily journal on the white space in scrap newspapers, giving me the scraps when I made my six visits to her. The last time I came, I was accompanied by Mr. Boune Young and another camp administrator. They allowed her to come past the gate section and into the conference room to meet with me.

Her hair had grown back to its original length and I could see that she had lost weight as she stood there in her prison uniform. She sat opposite Mr. Boune Young at the long, skinny wooden table. "I am well, thank you," she replied to his greeting.

"We care about you," Mr Boune Young told her as she started crying. "We will come here to be with you no matter what the judge decides and Bo will always be on your side. You did not do anything wrong, you are just crossing a fire-pit that is burning your feet," he said, and continued talking to her in a compassionate and supportive way. She glanced at me once in a while as her tears began to drip.

"You can move over and sit beside her," the administrator said. Larry put his arm across my shoulder and guided me over to her side while another woman stood up and pushed her chair over next to Nang Ya for me. I sat down, and she took my hand, wiped her eyes and smiled. "Thank you again for coming, all of you," she said, holding my hand tight.

"How often do you cut your hair?" she asked me, and everyone smiled. "Depends how often I get paid," I replied, "Since you left, I have to get my hair cut in the barber shop, maybe once a month, or once every two months, but I never like it as much as when you used to cut it for me." She smiled and everyone else laughed. I heard someone translating for Larry. Even the two guards at the door, who were constantly watching Nang Ya's movement, smiled at us.

She might have thought we would never have private time together, but she was sharing these private comments about me in a public meeting. "Do you need us to bring something?" Boune Young asked. "No, I am fine," she said. Mr. Boune Young took a handwritten sheet of paper out of his bag and laid it on the table. "The preliminary hearing is finished, the next scheduled court date is December, everyone here will be in the court-room," he said, "You might not see all of us while you are in the witness box, but I want you to know that we are with you." Then he offered her counseling.

"We have a Catholic priest in the camp," he told her, "if you want him to come for a visit, I will get you the required documents, and we could schedule it regularly if you like."

"Thank you for the offer," she replied, "but it is not necessary. If possible, I would like to see Bo weekly until the judge makes his final decision and I am condemned to death," she burst into tears again and stopped. The lawyer put his arm across her back.

"I will do everything in my power to stop such a sentence. Please don't give up on me too soon," he told her. "I wish at least one of my parents were here," she said. Everyone was silent for a moment. Then, Nang Ya glanced across at Larry. He smiled back at her.

"I want you to know, I am a friend of Bo's," he said. He looked at me curiously and asked, "Does she understand English?" He asked me. He continued. "Bo and I were always talking about you, and he is always missing you." She looked down at the floor.

"Thank you," she said, and looked straight at Boune Young, her tears trickling down beside her nose and reflecting the ceiling light. One of the guards brought a box of tissues, reaching over Nang Ya's shoulder to place them on the table in front of her.

"Thank you," she said again, then asked the guard if, when the meeting was over, she could talk to me privately, which he said she could. Larry stood up and walked over to Nang Ya, extending his hand to her. They shook hands and said "pleased to have met you."

When everyone began to walk out of the room to leave us alone together, the guard said, "Not here, we can take you back inside the gate and give you fifteen or twenty minutes together to talk." He guided us through the gate after the woman guard had put both of Nang Ya's hands in front of her and handcuffed them together. I followed them to the gate. The warden opened it and she passed through it, turning to face me.

"Can I give him a hug?" she asked. The woman guard replied that it would be inappropriate. Nang Ya walked over to the glass window and sat down. Still handcuffed, she reached down into her right-side pocket and pulled out a scrap of newspaper, handing it to me through a hole in the glass. The warden glanced at it, and I spread it out so he could look at it before I folded it up and put it in my pocket.

"I want to kiss you," she said, "The other night I dreamt that you came to the prison. For some reason I had a huge bed with egg-shell bed sheets and brown blankets. You made love to me endlessly." Her tears had dried, but her chin was red and her hands were shaking. "There is something I want to tell you," I said. She looked at me. "I know what you are going to tell me, but I just wanted to express myself, show you how I felt, and tell you about my dream. Please forgive me if what I said has offended you. How is she?" she asked. "She is fine. She is extremely jealous." Nang Ya looked at me again.

"Say hi to her for me, ok?" and that was all she said. She walked back to her cell as I stayed sitting there, watching until she disappeared. The warden called, "They are waiting for you outside." As I stood up, he asked to read Nang Ya's note. After reading it carefully, he tore it into pieces and threw them in the garbage. "You cannot bring it with you. If you visit again, it is not appropriate or safe for you to ask her for a note like this one." He pointed to the door.

On the trip back to camp, while the team was busy talking, I was writing down what Nang Ya had told me about the governor's business back in 1968 to '69, the two-year-period he was illegally involved in the Vietnam War before he was elected. When we arrived at the camp, I had written thirteen pages of notes.(but, I had never gotten the facts and details about what factories they were producing the bullet shells for)

"Are you writing a book or something, Bo?" Larry asked jokingly. As we continued teasing, I replied, "Maybe."

Soon after, I left the team and walked to my room, the strong gust of wind does sucking up the dust; as it moved away from the naked ground it hit the surrounding buildings and left a coating of dust on the walls and roofs. Everywhere looked red, as if it were red buildings from far away or even when one goes near them. People were covering their faces with whatever they were carrying.

When the wind stopped, I went to Tama rang forest, and for the rest of the day, I sat alone under a the forest t, re-arranging Nang Ya's diary, building it from the pieces of newspaper she had managed to give to me and from what she had told me. This is the last part of her diary that she had been giving to me from time to time.

The notes began stated back from 1968 and 1969, three years before the Secretary of State visited northern Vietnam for peace talks. He wanted the north to stop supporting the radicals in southern Vietnam, the United States were already established or renting the military air-base in Thailand, in Odon, to store its fighter jets, weapons and food supplies. A thirty-nine-year-old Mr. Boune Narane, a university professor, met with Captain Seng part five a military company in Laos about the empty bullet shell business.

According to the agreement, Seng would collect the shells, of all shapes and sizes, after bouts of fighting, and Boune Narane would sell them to private companies, which would produce something other house hole goods than bullets with them.

Because the bullets are made out of copper, they are valuable for things such as pots and pans and decorative items. but, the empty cells had to be collected from local soldiers, fighter jet pilots and residents of the areas where the fighting occurred, Seng had to pay those who would somehow risk their lives to bring them to him, with Boune Narane providing the money to him.

The second business was opium. The motive was work as fast as possible to get as much done as they could before the war ended, since then, civil law might be enforced not only in the Thai and Lao governments, but at international security check-points. The third business was prostitution, a business which did not require civil servants nor military personnel, but rather civilians or criminals, who would recruit good-looking women. The operation was to work in both countries; Lao and Thailand and provide services to soldiers fighting Communists in Laos as well as brothels in Laos and Thailand. Good candidates for recruitment were those who were poor and uneducated but good-looking. Virgins fetched a higher price from the rich customers. Captain Seng was also responsible for this.

Over the two-year period, the equivalent of 700 000 US dollars was spent in order to bring in 10 million dollars, which would then be invested in hotels, disco techs, bars and brothels across Thailand and Laos. This was to attract tourists: hippies and those who were living less morally would be served(she explained that the governor told her to know these detail to do her job better) and why was in US currencies estimation, until these days its remain unclear to me.

Boune Narane made his money from then on and used it for his political campaign. He was up for election in 1976, she told me. Now many brothels are his, but do not bear his name. Every time he travelled for official meetings or vacation, he also met with his business counterparts. I realised why he was attracted to Nang Ya, it was not only her good looks, as I had believed, it was also her education and her ability to work not only with her body, but her ability also including language skills, be able to work in Lao, Thai, English and French.

I put the notes back into my plastic bag and returned to my room. I went to the kitchen; Vana was sitting on a low stool in front of the stove, flipping fish.

"Looks like you and I will have supper alone again, B.," she said, "Searth is at the rotten house again." I knew that she meant the cock-fight hut. I sat down on the bamboo bench.

"It's ok," I said. "How were your day and your trip to the prison?" she asked, as she put the fish onto a plate and set it on the table. "I think we should eat first, I'll tell you all about it after supper," I said.

Night fell, and those unpleasant crickets started making noise again. It almost felt as though the humming of the crickets was part of my night life. I felt both annoyed and fascinated as my ears were occupied with the natural sound combined with human sounds. Our spoken words are a mixture of those insects, with their instinctual call that no human can understand, much as we cannot understand why we suffer. This time in my life did not feature sickness nor disease, but complication. It was the other, who had more power than I, who had complicated it in order to fulfill his desire, using his power to manipulate me. Thus, the complication had no logic, but crowded into my head repeatedly.

When I had finished telling Vana how my trip to the prison had gone, she cried. As usual, she offered to take me to see a monk, which I refused. She hesitated a moment, and then said, "you are too stubborn, Bo, at least listen to yourself once, you need to talk to a professional mind, you know that." I nodded, and then left to take a shower. When I returned with a brown towel around my waist and entered my room, Vana was sitting on my bamboo bed. I turned to the wall to put on my night wear, and she took the other smaller towel and stood behind me, trying to dry my hair. Then, she kissed my head to say good-night and left.

I had trouble sleeping. Nang Ya's words kept returning to my head—"I am dead inside, I dream about you, I want you to be there the hour I am hanged, I wish one of my parents were with me. Suddenly I heard the door slammed hard, almost like the whole hut was going to fall in.

"Vana! Wake up Bo and get out of the hut quick!" someone yelled from outside. I grabbed my jeans and ran outside wearing my undershirt and in bare feet. Searth and Vana were holding hands in front of my door and yelling at me to come out. I pushed my way through the door and we ran to safety in the field.

When we got to the field, it was crowded with people, with everyone talking, saying "It is done, we are done, it is done, it is over," and so forth. We saw the fire lighting up the east side of the camp, burning relentlessly toward our huts. We were helpless and hopeless as tricycles quickly gathered to bring water containers from the camp central well to the fire and trying to control it until dawn. The fire finally stopped just three huts away from ours. The section that had been burning was completely destroyed, along with people's belongings; luckily there were no deaths or injuries.

The next morning, the Nong Khai newspaper reported that the fire had started at 9 pm, and that communist underground workers were responsible. Everyone in the camp was frightened, not that the fire would burn again but of the underground communist workers. They crossed the border as refugees, working and spying on the old government regime's politics, and reorganizing militant armies to take back the country and destroying refugees' permanent residences to reduce the numbers escaping from Laos. The report, however, showed little apart from a photo of the burning huts and a couple of articles saying that those belonged to Hmong leader, who the article also claimed was a militia leader. Two days after the incident, the Hmong leader disappeared and his wife and daughters were taken to a refugee camp in the north of Thailand. Vana asked me to tell her the whole story from the article rather than reading it herself.

After we returned to our hut that morning, I could hear Vana making sounds and talking to herself as usual. Everything negative thing that happened to her and to the community was because of a sin someone had committed in a past life in her mind. The fact that her husband was addicted to gambling was due to the fact that she was unable to make an income. That afternoon, while all the adults were out helping those who were victims of the fire, Vana was walking from our hut to the location, back and forth, three times; she could not comprehend what to do. Meanwhile, many of the others were helping to set up new tents and lending cooking materials and sleeping items.

"If I had known this would happen, I would have been better off staying in my home country," she said. Before I could respond to her remark, she had walked away hesitantly. In truth,

I had great difficulty accepting her comments about sin. I found it senseless, but convincing to others who believe in superstition. It was a younger woman who told her that her parents had drowned while swimming across the Mekong and disappeared a year ago, but that now every night in her sleep, they came and brought her back home with them, and brought her back to the camp before dawn.

"My parents are no longer like they were when they were living, now they cannot tolerate the sun," she told Vana. As I listened to their conversation, the reality of the situation in their mind had root in a past life, rather than being explained by the facts of human error or temptation, as I was experiencing, losing someone because another has desires for her charms, that is a sin, isn't it? Listening to the conversation that bored me, I had no words to add, instead giving them a smile. When I started to walk away, the young woman's face lit up. "Don't worry," Vana told her, "Bo doesn't believe in anything he cannot see." I waved to them. "I might not come home for supper this evening, don't wait for me," I called to Vana.

Walking alone on a crowding street, I remembered what a monk had told me,"when a person caught a difficult time",

He said, their minds work harder and unnecessary thoughts occured in their heads." And I always remember that and believe it was not things that we learn nor teach, it just happening from fear and anxiety.

Chapter 24

I never felt confident about telling Valee about visiting Nang Ya in prison. I also had trouble making sense out of the fact that my feelings were shared between two women. Sometimes, this feeling did not seem to give me any real facts, it just burned and interrupted and disturbed my other thoughts, and sometimes I had thoughts that feelings of this kind should not take place in my life. I always had a kind of uncertain hope that some miracle would turn up, Nang Ya would get out of prison and get married, and that Valee's jealousy would end.

The reaction came right away, before I even had a chance to explain how the visit came about. "Is it necessary for you to visit her every second week?" Valee asked. She was holding a toothbrush in her right hand, and spitting out foam harshly without looking at me. "Yes," I said. "Don't give me your own invented words; it is you who wanted to!"

"No, they asked me to go."

"Who the hell, they, are you referring to?"

"The lawyer, camp director, and even Larry recommended it."

"Why?"

"Because I am a witness."

"Is that so, did you see when she killed her victim?"

"No, I didn't, but…"

"But what? What is wrong with you?" She walked into the other room to get changed. She stood in front of me, and pulled off her grey jogging pants and t-shirt so she was completely naked. She continued talking as she looked for her clothes. When she saw that my eyes had lit up, her mood changed a bit.

"By the way, I haven't had my monthly in over two months." I hugged and kissed her and ran my hand over her belly. "Thank god, I will be a dad!" I said, and finally she hugged me. "I am sorry, Bo, I was afraid to lose you that are what it is all about. I am not jealous because you visit her." Tears were running down both her cheeks.

At suppertime, Valee got the confirmation from her boss, the doctor, that she was in fact pregnant. That night, I felt that the whole world was perfect, that I would no longer be alone and lonely, I would finally have a family. A few days after I found out that Valee was pregnant, I decided that this phase of my life was transitional as we moved on to the next generation.

With our intellectual discussion, Valee accepted that the trips to the prison were part of my role without suspicion. However, I received a copy of a letter from the prison, which included a letter from Mr. Boune Young's letter saying that my behavious in accepting a note from a prisoner was unacceptable, and that I wouldn't be allowed to see her anymore, since I was not her husband. The witness was only needed on trial day.

On the day Valee and I moved in together, I felt embarrassed. She was right, from the beginning; it was I who had asked Larry for help to get permission to visit Nang Ya in prison for my own personal reasons. There was never a reason given to me to go to the prison as a witness. Valee never complained or argued with me each time I went to a trial. I never confessed my failure and ignorance to her, which gave me guilt through our relationship.

My baby was born in good health in September, 1979, six months later, in February, 1980, we were brought to Canada. Before we moved to Canada, Larry moved to the south of Thailand to work in a Cambodian refugee camp in Thailand near the Thai-Cambodian border.

A week before we left for Canada, Mr. Boune Young came to our hut. "There is something I would like you to know," he told me. "At the last trial, Nang Ya wasn't brought to the court. Her lawyer said that she had disappeared during the night without a trace. The Nong Khai governor, Mr. Boune na rane, was under investigation for bribery and giving permission to local bars, restaurants and brothels to establish their businesses without permits." He told me not to worry and to stay in hiding, though I was free to go out with friends and wait for the departure date.

We were not married. The fact that we had had our baby made people see us as a married couple, not just a couple. From the day Valee gave birth, Vana never mentioned her name when she wanted to leave a message for her, just saying 'your wife.' On my last day of teaching Vana English, she made a nice cake and told me not to eat it until I got home; wrapping the cake in banana leaves. "Here, Bo!" she said. "Bring this cake to your wife, but make sure she gives you a piece!"

That happy time lasted about few months. Then the thing I could never have imagined arrived. A week before our date to go to the airport, I received a letter from the Bay area in California in the United States. The letter was typed, had no signature or returns address, and said "Congratulations with your new wife and newborn baby. You were right, miracles can happen!" The stamp on the envelope was marked January 14, 1980. Immediately all thoughts, connections and temptations I had ostracized from my mind returned. To ignore the past, I felt like I would just have been a liar; the truth was that feelings would never go away from the one who experienced them. But, to keep this new relationship and family, one has to learn to practice new thoughts.

Valee never knew of my internal suffering. She was as happy as I should have been from the day our child was born. Afterward, I had a father's thoughts. I counted the days since my child had been born, and the days became weeks, months became years, and I cannot wait to hear the baby's first word to call me (daddy). As for the rest of the time, Valee had become the best friend I had ever had. She managed the family quite well, preparing to cope with the cold temperatures as we had known through reading and to adapting to the new culture. Most importantly, we were preparing ourselves to be employed. We were both starting to read about the Western lifestyle in magazines and listening to international radio broadcasts (The Voice of America) in which it provided language we understand better.

As a matter of fact, I never embraced the feelings of the past. It remained on its own in me, the more I tried to forget it, the more vividly it returned to my mind, clouding my daily minds that influenced my behaviors sometime spite. I had less desire to sleep with Valee. "Do you find I am fat?" she asked. "No, I am sorry, it is not that."

"What is it, then?"

"I don't know."

"Do you want me to talk to the doctor?"

"Not necessary. I think once we get to Canada, things should return to the way they were."

"Why is that?"

"Maybe it has to do with the anxiety, of wanting to get out of here."

"Maybe you're right, I thought that too for the sake of our baby."

As she breast-fed, Valee's breasts got larger and filled with milk. When it came time to feed, she squeezed some off first and then let our son suck; inviting me to watch the way the baby drank the milk.

There were many things Valee worried about with our baby. Many children in the camp were affected by some sort of skin disease, dry and purple on their legs, arms and feet. Many were caused by lack of nutrients, and there were other infections which we did not have the information to identify. I felt lucky that Valee was a nurse, even though there was a lack of medicine, she managed to take care of our basic needs. But, the more we had opportunities and felt lucky, the guiltier we felt. We had witnessed children dying every day. Due to these circumstances, Valee began to realize that my downturn was from the reality of the environment.

The Canadian commercial flight left Don Meuang airport at midnight in February, 1980. Over 200 passengers boarded the flight, all were refugees; Cambodian, Vietnamese, and Laotian. The flight would go from Bangkok to Tokyo then to Vancouver. And that was the sky route for the Canadian international flight, I learn later.

Valee sat beside the window, our baby in her arms. She puts her arms across my back to guide me to look out the window with her. "It is interesting," she said. She looked out the window with her face in a dream. I took comfort in her and the baby.

"Things will be ok," I said. And from time to time we looked out the window again, wanting to land in a destiny we now knew. Passing through the air above the clouds, my mind had no set, just like a moving cloud, my destination was no destiny. Valee held my arm as her eyes closed, leaning her head on the comfortable seat as she went to sleep with the baby still on her arm.

Alone in the world, in my mind, I heard the sound of the flowing Mekong River. I saw it again, the abandoned shore, the place I found myself away from the criminals after I arrived on the other side of the Mekong river in Thailand, waiting for the sun to rise as I began a search for safety. And then, the woman who saved my life while risking her own, saying "I will be with you forever, dead or alive." Her voice brought some hope to me that, some day, I would see her again in bay area California, alive and well. I had no clear understanding why she risked her life to save mine. As I was about to talk to her, she disappeared into the midst of the ocean all the while whispering "you're right, miracles can happen." As I was going to ask her of the location where she lived, I heard baby cry.